Her lips still there, still on his … soft … gentle, soothing, telling Chris everything would be okay, saying *I'm here for you. I'll help you. I … I …*

Jess pulled away.

Oh no, she thought when she saw his eyes. *I've ruined everything.*

Also by James Steimle

Fiction
The Kukulkan Manuscript
The Ghost People
The Room That Wasn't There

(Writing as Jim Blackstone)
Interference

(For Children)
The Autumn Land

Nonfiction
Multicultural Instruction
Forgotten Forerunners
Myths and Legends
Fire in the Desert
Der Geist ist Willig

(For Children)
An Elementary History of the World

FEW ARE CHOSEN

by
James Steimle

Technical Data Freeway, Inc.

Technical Data Freeway, Inc.
P.O. Box 308, Poway, CA 92074
Visit www.tdfbooks.com

Previously published by Osiris Publications © 2004 by James Michael Steimle

Minor editorial changes have been made for this edition.

ISBN-13: 978-0-9841600-2-0
ISBN-10: 0-9841600-2-7

Printed in the United States of America

This book is set in Adobe Garamond

For

ShaLayne and Lee Evans,
Stacy and Eric Anderson,
Jamie and Eugene Casados,

grand romantics all

There are many called, but few are chosen.
And why are they not chosen? Because ...
they do not learn this one lesson ...

Doctrine and Covenants 121:34-35

FEW ARE CHOSEN

Chapter One

Jess licked away the spot of mustard from her upper lip and glanced at Chris, hoping he hadn't noticed. She grinned a silent *Thank you* at Tamara Cline, the best friend a girl could ever have, and Tam blinked once over her soda to say *You're welcome.*

"So there's these three devils, okay? They approach the Big Man—a sort of judgment for the demonic kind. The Boss says to the first, a big ugly dude with horns and hair and fangs all over—" Tam grinned at Dave. "Not you, Hulk Meister."

"Ha, ha," he said and sipped his root beer.

"The Boss says, 'What did you all do today to ruin mankind?'"

In the pinched voice of one of these demons, Dave interrupted. "Well, Master Man, I told belabored seminary fables on a stormy spring night to make members of the Church feel guilty."

With another smile, Tam patted Dave on the arm. She had already mentioned that he would have heard this story in seminary today, had he bothered to attend. "I'm not sharing this with *you*, Dave. Chris here hasn't been to seminary in almost a year. And Jess—"

"Who is Catholic and probably doesn't even care," said Dave.

"—Jess … likes my stories, don't you, girl."

Beaming, Jess looked over her hamburger at Chris who, chomping away, seemed to notice nothing but his double cheese with bacon. Yet he nodded at Tam. "Go on."

"See?" Tam said to Dave. "Anyway, so this first devil tells the Boss, 'I got a teenager to start crystal meth today.'"

Dave sucked hard on his straw and rolled his eyes.

Her hands jumped through the air as she gave life to the ghouls in her story. "'Good, good!' says the Big Man, who then turns to the second devil. 'And what, my great, smelly apparition of delight, did *you* do today?'

"'Why,' says the second freak, 'I got a drug addict a job selling meth to everybody!'

"'My!' says the Boss. 'That certainly is *fine* work, you capital meister, you! But I've got to tell you both, little funky Demon Bob here—'"

Dave raised his hands. He didn't wait to be called on. "Did Brother Anderson really call the third devil Bob?"

Chris smiled a little.

A wave of warmth, as well as hope, hummed through Jess's muscles, though she pretended not to pay special notice to Chris's actions at all. He glanced at her. Lightning.

Leaning toward his buddy, Dave whispered, "That's why I cut out seminary when I can. Too much *funky* business, if you ask me."

"I never missed a day," said Chris slurping from his cup. His eyes stroked Jess's face for a moment. "Not even when I was sick."

Am I staring at him?! Jess gagged away in shame. *I am!*

Dave held up his cup of Coke. "Going to school even when you're ill, I must say, *is* sick."

Tam put her food down and bared her palms. "No more story? Anyone?" She slapped the table unintentionally. "That's fine."

"*I* want to know the end," said Chris. He glanced at Jess again.

Why? she thought. *Did he have some missionary goal in this? Or had he caught her eyes gawking yet* again? Jess cowered over her plate: *He'll never speak to me.*

"The end's simple," said Dave.

Tam dropped her mouth open and whooped, her red hair bouncing for a moment in a natural way that Jess's never would.

"The last devil's done better than the rest. Forget the drugs, that's for losers," he said.

All eyes met each other in a secretive communiqué: Dave had been known to loiter with friends who could tell you everything about illegal addictions. Sure he and Chris had been friends forever, because they regularly shared classes at church. But while Chris was old for his age and had graduated from high school a year ahead of the rest of the crowd, Dave had been held back a year, which made him the most ancient student in Harmon High—the only guy who had started the school year with a draft card *in his pocket.*

"Without anyone from either side realizing it," Dave said, "*Bob* has set up a whole franchise of *churches* across the United States. Behind the pulpit of each one, he's stuck a dirty minister. The priest raises his arms before his congregation each Sunday, peers into a Bible or some other book he picked up in college, then tells the congregation exactly what the little Devil Bob has told him to say."

"Which is?" said Chris.

Dave grinned around the straw in his mouth. "Keep the commandments … "

The burger shop drew silent, magnifying the sound of other patrons and an old song by Richard Marx playing from the loudspeakers.

"That's it?" said Jess, totally lost if this Mormon story was supposed to have a moral.

Tam glared at the Hulk Meister.

"Keep the commandments," Dave said, "… *tomorrow.*"

Chris harrumphed. He smiled with his eyes as he thought about the tale and bit into his dinner.

Tam pulled her chin into her neck, taking a minute to run over Dave's impressive and unpredictable wisdom. "*That's* not how the story goes."

Still not understanding, but certain the meaning was clear to the rest of them, Jess played the logic through: *Keeping commandments was good, right? It was what "dis-*

ciples" were supposed to do.

Ah!

Putting it off ... *well, that would be wrong, wouldn't it? Kind of like a serial killer saying he won't slay another human ... after today.*

Tam raised her sculpted eyebrows. She sighed. "Your version is a lot better than Brother Anderson's."

"Which was?" said Jess.

"Oh, the third devil got a dealer to make the drug himself before passing it out in heaps to other dealers."

"Not as good as what I said," said Dave.

"Dave!" Tam gasped. She steadied herself on the edge of the small table, shared eyes with everyone, then giggled. "I think I've discovered your *calling* in life: the Church Educational System!"

Even Chris laughed at that. The image was too hard for any of them to picture, including Jessica Singer, who had never sat in one of those early-morning classes but heard about them time and again—Dave in a white shirt and tie wearing that beat-up, blue and gold letterman's jacket he never took off? His little cross country pin sparkling before a room of pious Latter-day Saints!

She chuckled and peeked up again at Chris.

"Yeah." Dave swabbed ketchup off of the hand holding his burger and poked the lathered finger into his mouth. "Maybe after an angel knocks me off my feet and does the whole Alma-unconscious thing to me."

Jess shifted in her seat. She hadn't agreed to come so

she could listen to all this LDS bantering. Over and over, Chris seemed to be forgetting that he was eating next to anyone. Had his strong blue eyes not radiated so much *innocence* as he stared out the window and into the faint mist of approaching night rain, Jess would have been sure that Chris was trying to avoid her altogether.

After what happened at the Valentine's Day dance, her eagerness had mixed with hopelessness and turned her stalwart poise to a sort of spinning mush. She didn't know where she stood anymore.

Erupting into laughter for the hundredth time, Tam poked a fingernail into one of Dave's massive shoulders. "Can you *believe* that joke Brother Anderson told on Monday?!" It was a story Dave actually had been present to hear. "A copperhead? And a *fish*!" She banged his arm with a fist and laughed twice as loud.

More inside jokes, thought Jess.

Lettuce and flakes of cheese from Dave's hamburger rained onto the short yellow table.

"Hey!" Dave barked, lifting his other hand and cocking his head. "Watch the side of beef, okay? I don't want to have to scrape my dinner off the floor before I eat it. They don't clean places like this, you know!"

One of the employees passed at that very moment. Smelling of burger grease and fries, he gave Dave a dirty glance that bent the Hulk Meister over his soda straw.

When it was safe, everybody but Jess cracked up.

"Oh, I see." Brave at last, she wiped her hands with a

napkin and cleared her throat. "More Mormon talk, eh? Well it's pretty easy for me to tell when a good Catholic girl isn't wanted."

Listing, bumping elbows with the giant senior she "wasn't" dating, Tam sniggered, reached out a hand, and tapped Jess's arm as if the appendage were a small pet. "Sorry, girl. Not trying to leave you out at all."

But Tam couldn't stop laughing, and it had to be about the joke only she and Dave had heard, because the Blaine's Burger employee's look hadn't been that funny.

Rolling her eyes, Jess said, "That's all right. Chris obviously didn't hear the your copperhead fish story either."

As if permitted now, she squinted at Chris and his loose brown hair for a few seconds.

"And he doesn't seem to care anyway."

At the dance, Jess had *felt* that hair. She had felt a lot of things.

Rather than staring at the tabletop as he ate, Chris Noble, who had been the tall quiet type in high school before graduating ahead of the rest of the crowd, focused on the darkness beyond the window.

A light patter of ran hit the street in scattered droplets.

Dave gnawed into his burger. "*What* are you gawking at?"

Jess recoiled, embarrassed. Then she found Dave frowning at Chris instead of her.

What does it matter, Jess thought. *Chris isn't ogling me, is all. And I guess that's my answer tonight.*

She examined her food. Hidden tears clogged her throat.

This was supposed to be a date, of sorts anyway. Though Chris sat here in the flesh, his mind wandered somewhere in the unexpected rain. Tam had organized the entire thing, and now even she turned to gaze out the window.

Over and over in classes the previous year, Tam had leaned to Jess's ear and whispered, "Chris is staring at you again!" Of course, whenever she had turned to see, his eyes flitted away, usually to the ceiling or the floor. They had never gotten together, though Jess was certain he had showed interest now and then. Jess blamed Rita Hirsch, Chris's last girlfriend. Something had happened that made him stay away from all females, like he was frightened even while interested. If he had ever revealed his feelings to a single soul, only Dave would know the truth. And Dave wasn't about to spill it.

Sighing at Tam, Jess glanced at the glass door.

Beyond it, she could see Dave's green Toyota Tacoma parked under the blue and yellow light of the Blaine's Burger sign. The dimmed lights from the closed flower shop sparkled beyond the car. Dave had provided the transportation. A ride was the only excuse Tam came up with to force her favorite thug to come along.

Dave was Chris's best friend too. He therefore provided Chris the necessary moral support, against what was supposed to be a covert operation, code name: CHESS (Tam had pointed out to him that *Ch*ris plus J*ess* made *Chess*).

Tam and Dave had agreed that Jess and Chris would

look *fine* together.

So they were all out as "friends" this evening.

What girl wanted to be just "friends" when Mr. Perfect finally appeared?

But until Dave finished eating and got antsy, this dead-end date wasn't going to reach a finish line any time soon.

Wait a second, Jess thought.

Now *everyone* was leaning at the window.

In the silence, Jess noticed the flexing muscles in Chris's neck and jaw. And his brown hair again—he had the sort of thick hair that never needed mousse, gel or spray. Just a little water, and that dark softness ran in waves over his *fine* ears.

Jess rolled her eyes to clear her vision.

No one moved.

So she then she said, "Okay, what's all the hubbub, bub?"

A streetlight stuck out of the ground a good stone's throw away along Sunrise Boulevard. Blaine's Burger hunkered at the eastern outskirts of the quiet Southern California community in which they lived. Across both lanes lay nothing except a deep ditch of flowing rainwater from the mountain range to their left and black fields, beyond the gutter, racing out to a string of house lights which stretched like a long white line of cars in the distance.

"What is it?" said Jess.

Tam whipped around and leaned into the table. "Oh, it's nothing. French fry?"

When Tam said something was *nothing*, she was always covering something of great interest.

Jess sat straight and lifted her head high.

Then she saw them on the right.

Two young men with cropped hair, sharp chins, white shirts, and dark ties flapping under one arm as they rode bicycles in the drizzle—if you would call *that* riding.

One guy spoke over his shoulder, chuckling it seemed against the warm rain spraying the side of his face.

The other, in the rear, shook his head. His mouth moved. Though pedaling slowly on the other side of the road and coming this way, they were too far for Jess to even try and read their lips.

"Ah. I see. Attack of the Mormons, is it?" said Jess. She put up her hands. "I'm surrounded. I give, I give! Just don't shoot."

Nobody laughed.

The missionary in the lead swerved as he gazed back, talking.

Passing beneath the yellow streetlight, he careened a second time and would have pulled right into traffic had there been any. Almost drunk with the heat of his conversation, he corrected again, yelling back to his companion something almost loud enough to hear through the steadily increasing rain and the distance and the glass of Blaine's Burger shop.

"French fry? Did you say yes?" Humming a note, Tam dropped her remaining bag of potato bits next to Jess's hamburger. "I'm stuffed. You can have 'em all. So, Chris …!"

Jess didn't look at the food. She glanced at Chris,

whose adams apple bobbed once as he swallowed.

Dave's voice was hardly a whisper. "Guy's gonna get himself killed."

Then the missionary vanished.

Chapter Two

Chris lurched out of his seat. Not to help, but to get a better look.

The missionary had shot right off the road and into the five-foot ditch that ran between the asphalt and the endless fields.

His companion slowed. He coasted by under the yellow lamp. He laughed as he passed the missionary in the ditch.

Drifting by the burger shop right across the street, he squealed the bike brakes, almost stopping, and shouted for the other guy to get out of the water because his clothes were getting soaked.

Jess made out that much. At this hour, they couldn't possibly have any more appointments. Most likely, she thought, the missionaries lived in the Azul Terrace Apartments less than a block past the burger shop, which meant they were going home.

The fallen missionary's head rose, then one shoulder and another.

His mouth moved: *This isn't very funny.* He said something else, but the roar of an engine and a flash of yellow color buried the last of his words.

Tam screamed.

Jess had to collect the pieces and replay them in her mind to realize what was happening:

She had blinked at the missionary who waited for his companion.

He had stopped and faced the fallen guy, who brayed out of the gutter twenty-five feet behind him.

Then he too had disappeared.

An old Chevy, the yellow car with the loud engine, erased him completely, then drove the left front corner straight into the ditch.

The back of the car raised into the air, hung crooked and stayed that way.

Dave flew from his seat and rushed behind Chris, who had already rung the bell hanging from the glass door.

Tam held both hands over her mouth. A squeak and a whimper escaped her throat.

Jess gasped and started to run.

All four Blaine's Burger employees made it to the door before her. She crammed her way through the bottleneck to find Chris and Dave across the street.

They pointed, giving orders to one another with their eyes, then dropped into the flowing ditch.

The rain fell a little harder, roaring on the pitched side of the yellow Chevy.

The other missionary left his bicycle and climbed onto the asphalt with trembling arms. Heaving himself upright, he uttered something that sounded too much like Tam's squeak and whimper. Hunched forward and open-mouthed, the missionary navigated the wet weather in the direction of the accident.

The rain hammered thick droplets at high speed.

From the cab of the automobile, a driver kicked the door open so that it pointed like a flat hand in the direction of the increasing storm. "Got in my way!" The driver slipped out and down, landing his feet on the edge of the road. "Stupid Mormon shirt blinded me!"

Jess almost tripped as she gazed into the ditch.

In two-and-a-half feet of rushing water, Chris held the victim's face out of the current by the base of the neck.

Jess remembered flashes of data from her health class: accident; neck; stretcher. "You can't move the body!"

Chris gave her a quick nod. To use his own head as a small umbrella, he leaned over the floating missionary. The rain splattered into Chris's soaking hair as he fumbled his fingers for a pulse and lowered his ear to listen for breathing.

It didn't take an A-student like Jess or even a meteorologist to realize the little river they stood in was rising fast. Chris saw this and glanced at Jess once more.

They *couldn't* leave him there.

The missionary didn't make a single sound. His eyes didn't open when the second missionary swayed next to Jess, muttering, "Comp? Comp?! Oh, man." He brushed brown water out of one eye with the heel of his hand.

The teetering Chevy seemed to slide a bit, the right

front corner sinking a couple inches into the water and the far embankment made of earth. Or maybe it was only an illusion caused by the rising swell.

"Dave?!" shrieked Tamara, who had gathered at the edge of the road with the rest of the crowd.

Facedown, Dave floated in the thundering rush of gutter water. With his shoulder caught against the undercarriage of the car and his legs and arms lost in the current, he looked like a corpse that had died too quickly.

Then he came up with a scream. He glanced at his shoulder and at the Chevy's hot engine casting up steam as the water fought to cool the metal. Turning eyes to Chris, he said, "He's not pinned. We gotta get him out of here."

"We can't move the body!" Chris shouted.

"We won't be able to stand up in this for long! He's getting buried."

Chris jerked his face to where Jess stood in the rain. "911!"

She mouthed the numbers. A moment later, she said, "Right!" Though someone else *had to* have called, already, she pulled her cell phone from a pocket.

As soon as a nasal sound started talking on the other end, Jess said, "There's been an accident! East Sunrise in front of Blaine's Burger! He's hurt!!!"

Whatever the woman on the other end asked, Jess didn't hear.

The phone fell from her hands as Chris and Dave heaved the unconscious missionary upward. She took one arm. The other missionary grabbed a leg. Tam reached, as did the hands of the Blaine's Burger employees. They pulled on the missionary's flesh, skeleton, and church clothes together, setting him with care on the side of the road.

A car stopped and hit its flashers.

Help at last! Jess thought.

An old woman shambled out of the driver's side and stood under an orange and black umbrella. "Oh! Oooh!"

Great! Jess turned away, opening wide her eyes. What are we doing?!?

They were breaking every rule of lifesaving she had ever learned in Health.

Shake the body and say, Annie! Annie!

What of spinal cord injuries? What about broken arms or legs? "Is he breathing?" she said. No one heard her.

No, she thought. *He's dying.*

But then, Chris and Dave had been Boy Scouts—something she had poked fun at last year. She hoped they knew what they were doing.

Maybe somewhere in the Scout Handbook it said, *Moving the victim of an accident is permissible in the event that a deep-water current may drown or crush him before Emergency Medical Technicians arrive.*

She thought the text unlikely.

She shook her head, couldn't think straight, and then realized her cell phone was missing.

Had she even called 911?

Jess couldn't remember.

"Oh yes, right, I did," she said to herself, but couldn't

recall the conversation.

In the white glow of the new headlights, Chris spoke in his typical no-nonsense voice to his friend. "Get the umbrella."

"Here," said Dave, reaching toward the old woman who had stopped. "Let's have that."

The grandmother gulped and shook her head.

Dave stood, charged her, locked his fingers around the thin metal pole and stared her down. "Get in your car if you don't want to get wet."

Releasing the umbrella, the old woman hummed a sound of terror. She did so over and over in the rain, then retreated into her vehicle.

Dave covered Chris and the other missionary as they crouched over the unconscious young man in the water-logged white shirt.

"Where are their coats?" said Jess. Shivering, from shock mostly, she blinked against the rain and looked at Tam. "Don't missionaries listen to the weather?"

"It's not like they watch television, Jess," Tam snapped.

That confused Jess even more.

Six minutes later, Dave cried, "Where's that ambulance?!"

Faces stared up and down the street, searching, listening as visibility continued to drop with the cloudburst.

Jess heard rain and the river and a distant pound of thunder.

"This isn't happening," said Jess, realizing that through it all, she watched Chris, a hero with every breath, ignoring his sidekick Dave. This was supposed to be their date, Operation Chess, remember? Tam promised romance at last. She tramped around for her phone.

The ditch water blasted into the nose of the Chevy and its undercarriage.

The current had risen.

She was certain now: If the missionary had stayed put, he would have drowned.

Kneeling beside his companion, the other missionary shuddered. Then, drumming his fingers on his face and brow, he lifted his chin. He reached into one pocket and withdrew a small key ring.

From the ring, only two keys hung. There was also a little brass doodad—for decoration, Jess supposed.

Tamara jerked her head back, drawing a short intake of breath.

The missionary with the keys was talking to himself. "I should …" He licked his lips.

Chris and Dave exchanged glances.

"Oil?" said Chris.

Jess rubbed the water off her face. "What did he say?"

No one answered her.

The missionary's face burst suddenly with a tiny smile that took him straight back to weeping. "You an elder?"

"For four days," said Chris, with a slight nod of the head.

Jess saw the uncertainty and determination in the firm muscle and bone of his face.

Dave hardened his jaw. He stood and puffed out his

massive chest. "All right, everyone. How about a little space here, okay?!!"

Bodies rocked, but no one left the scene. Not even the driver, who paced in the downpour, swearing and shouting into the air.

Rolling the fingers of his free hand into a square fist, Dave growled at the burger employees. His eyes said it all: He intended to pummel anyone who wanted to stick around.

"Back off, people!" said Tam, swinging about. "Let's give them some air until the paramedics finish their coffee and decide to show up."

Hardly thinking anymore about traffic, the onlookers retreated to the far side of the street or back to their cars—more autos had stopped and lined up. The girls remained where they stood.

Dave had not shooed everyone away for *air*.

He crouched over Chris and the two missionaries again, holding the orange and black shield low to block as much rain as possible.

The sky lit up, went dark.

Thunder boomed directly above them

"What's going on?" Jess said, still shivering.

Beneath the orange and black umbrella, the old woman's headlights reflected off of both missionaries' white shirts, bathing Chris, Dave, and the two strangers in a brilliant glow magnified by the potency of rain.

Tam gave Jess a tug. As they started to drift across the street, the pinpoint of white light behind them began to grow hazy. Like a vision of heaven seen through a small window in a dream, the light seemed to grow brighter.

Despite the water running over her face, Jess could still see plenty.

Chris took the missionary's keys. He fiddled with them, unscrewing a part of the brass decoration.

"Jess," said Tam, putting hands onto her shoulders. "You're soaked through. Take a look. You can see right through that shirt, girl. Let's get you inside."

She blinked down. "Yes. Okay. You're right." Crossing both arms over her chest, Jess stared around Tam's shoulders as their backward footfalls carried them farther and farther away from the mysterious scene.

Tam's eyes burned with intensity, though she only looked back at the accident one time—at the four figures glowing under an umbrella beside a car sticking out of a ditch with one door opened and aimed like a cannon at the dumping sky.

Chris lifted his hands.

Though they trembled, he settled them onto the head of the unconscious missionary.

He opened his mouth.

As his slow words drowned in the storm, Jess was able to make out the first part.

"Elder Richard Smith. In the name of our Savior, Jesus Christ, and by the power of the holy Melchizedek Priesthood which I hold … "

A little faster, they pushed backward through the short

parking lot.

"Tamara!" Jess whispered. She couldn't stop shivering.

Her friend knocked the bell as she shoved at the door to the burger shop. "Just wait, girl. Everything will fine."

* * *

Two minutes later, the ambulance pulled up. The white and orange vehicle blocked their view and flashed red lights around them.

Jess and Tam ran across the road with everybody else. Dave could kill them all later if he wanted to. He otherwise allowed the intrusion.

The EMTs surrounded the unconscious missionary, pushing the other three guys into the rain with invisible hands.

Dave returned the old woman's umbrella.

She kept it in her car next to her, the doors locked.

A police cruiser splashed water as it stopped behind the ambulance. Blue, red, yellow lights flashed, reflecting from everything, including every single water droplet. The smell of exhaust slid through the rain, which had started to thin out a bit.

The officer took a moment to climb out of the car. When he did, he started listening to people—not that he had much choice. Everyone had something to say, especially the second missionary and the mad driver of the Chevy. Both started yelling, so the officer had to raise his hands and speak louder.

As the EMTs positioned the victim onto a stretcher and rolled him into the back of the ambulance, Chris whistled at the missionary talking with the cop. He shouted. "Time to go!"

The missionary took two steps before the officer caught him. "No sir, you can see him at the hospital. Now, you say *you* went in the ditch first?"

The driver of the Chevy threw both hands in the air. "That guy swung out right in front of me! In the rain! He just plain yanked his bike left! Right into my lane! And his soaked white shirt acted like a mirror to my headlights! Blinded me—"

The officer told him to wait his turn.

The driver never once stopped spilling out colorful details in his defense. The more he talked, the more creative he got.

"*I'll* tell you what happened!" said Tam, marching over there. "I saw the *whole* thing."

The officer pointed a pen at her. "Get out of the rain! I'll take all of your statements in the restaurant."

Dave caught the EMT before he could shut the backdoor of the ambulance.

The EMT cocked his head to one side. "We got to roll now, kid, or this guy's history."

Reaching for Chris's jacket, Jess opened her mouth to ask what had happened, what was happening.

With Tam away, she stood in the rain more alone than

ever.

As she reached, the missionary with the cop shook his head at Chris.

Slipping from her fingers before she could catch a hold onto the drenched shirt clinging to his muscles, Chris drew a fast gulp of air and took a step towards the ambulance,

Dave bounced his eyes from the missionary to Chris and then to the open ambulance door he held while the EMT tried to pull it shut. To Chris, Dave said, "I'll go." In a single motion, he reached into the pocket of his letterman's jacket and flung his keys.

Chris snatched them out of the air. "I'll stay with the other elder. We'll track you down."

With a groan, the EMT released the door and shook his head. "All right. Get in, then."

Dave nodded once more to Chris before shutting himself inside the ambulance.

Then finally, Chris turned to Jess.

Stepping right up to her, he put his face close enough to kiss.

Right here, right now, she would no longer feel the rain if those full lips touched hers.

Contact!

She held her breath.

Chris stared directly into her soul, his eyes so blue she felt the sun come out and announce summer vacation forever. "Jess?"

Her eyes blinked as she looked through the rain into

his. She tried to speak through a suddenly raspy throat. "Yes?"

Without peeking downward, his fingers touched her left hand and opened it. He pushed Dave's car keys into her palm. "I'm really sorry about tonight. I … Take the truck. I have a feeling Elder Rutter and I will get a ride with Officer Arrest Everybody over there."

"What?" she said, swallowing, her mind hearing one thing, her heart longing for different words.

Standing this close to him, she thought she felt his warmth. She smelled his Chrome cologne. And the look of the water running down his face and over his mouth almost made her knees buckle.

But what did he say? Her head spun.

"Get Tam … and go home."

He dove through the hard-falling rain toward the missionary, the officer, and the furious driver of the yellow Chevy.

She waited.

Chris didn't look back once.

Chapter Three

Jess got into Dave's Tacoma and sneezed all over the steering wheel. Leaning her head back, she shut her eyes. "Please don't tell anyone I just did that."

"Doesn't matter." Tamara stared through the back window at the accident. "We're dripping all over the seats anyway. Are we going?"

Jess listened to the constant drum roll of rain on the hood and roof of the cab. With the sleeve of her shirt, she dabbed at her face to stop the water from dripping off the edge of her nose. It wasn't very lady-like, but she sat safe in the knowledge that all the boys had fled from sight. "You're being awfully evasive."

"No." Tam pulled down the sun visor to check her makeup and hair in the tiny mirror hiding there. "You just haven't put the keys in the ignition yet."

Squinting in the dim light from the blue and yellow BLAINE'S BURGER sign shining in the rain above the truck, Jess settled her hands on the steering wheel. She squeezed the rubber until it squeaked under her skin. "What happened back there?"

"I *know*! Can you *believe* it? Wait until we tell Ben! He'll kick himself for missing everything. I told him to call in sick and come with us. He hates hearing about stuff second-hand. I need some gum." Tam rummaged through her purse.

Jess shook her head. "That's not what I'm talking about."

Smiling, Tam didn't bother looking up. "Trust me girl. *You* need some gum. Maybe burgers wasn't such a good idea."

"You're not going to tell me." Jess sighed. "That's fine." She blinked at the windshield. She watched the rivulets of water running down the glass like transparent worms trying to escape the rain.

"Don't feel bad about Chris." Tam continued her search, ever deeper into her black bottomless bag. Car keys, attached to about thirty exotic key rings, hung from the strap and jingled, nonstop Christmas bells competing with the evening storm.

"Chris?" Jess turned in her seat. She searched the cars across the street, the wandering emergency people, but didn't see Chris anymore.

Other cop cars had stopped. Officers threw burning red flares onto the road to divert traffic.

With yellow lights flashing, a tow truck slowed and stopped next to one officer. The driver pointed at different sides of the trashed Chevy. He seemed to be shouting to be heard through the storm. The policeman shook his head and waved a hand in another direction.

"I hear some guys just go through these cycles, you know?" Tam nodded while speaking. "Take my older brother. He's married and moved to Austin. Once in a while when he visits, I get to sit with his wife, and *she* has told me a thing or two, let me say, sister!"

Jess raised a hand. "Tam."

"Like, one time she sat with their baby—the *cutest* little bald-headed boy you *ever* saw; he'll grow into his hair, I hear—and she *told* me, Gustav just doesn't even see her some days. His *presence* changes her into the invisible woman, or a piece of furniture!"

"Tamara," said Jess, shutting her eyes.

"But other days, my brother's a saint. Always helping with the baby. Always cleaning up the dishes or vacuuming their apartment or gassing up her car and getting it washed for no special reason."

"Hon." Jess placed a hand on her best friend's forearm.

"My point is, Chris is probably at the low part of an ever-hidden male monthly cycle. Like if he was a woman, he would be—"

"Forget about it." Jess gave Tam's arm a gentle squeeze.

"*Why can't I find any stupid gum!!!*" Tam heaved handfuls of makeup—lip liner, eyeliner, extra cover-up, lipsticks, chapsticks, oil pads, rouge, and mascara—as well as a couple pens, a fuzzy cat toy, the stub of a movie ticket, an MP3 player, a rubber candy cane left over from Christmas, and a red spider ring Dave had tossed at her—and she had willingly caught!—the day after Halloween. And just as fast as she lifted all these bits of treasure and garbage, she flung them back into her purse with a crash that sent the spider to the floor and an unmentionable sanitary object chasing hard after it.

"It's okay, Tamara!" Jess lifted her other hand to calm her down. She caught both of Tam's hands and held them still against the purse. "This … is just a passing thing, is all."

"I'm sorry." Tam wept with downcast eyes. "It's all my fault."

"No, it isn't."

"I'm always playing the matchmaker and failing like Emma in that Jane Austen novel."

Despite earning A's—except in history, which she hated with a livid passion—Jess hadn't read the book, but she remembered the movie. She patted her friend's knuckles, then pulled Tam's head to her shoulder. "Not important."

"It's just, you two looked so *happy* together at the dance." A smile broke through as she sniffed in tears. "Even though you guys left the church foyer *only* when the chaperones came to see who was loitering in the shadows."

Clearing her throat, Jess remembered that wonderful night last month.

It had been the Valentine's Day dance at the Mormon church—the Stake Center, Tam had called it—on Colville Road.

Chris hadn't planned on going. It was four days before

he was turning nineteen and would no longer be able to attend "these" dances for some reason.

He didn't have a girlfriend anymore.

In a fit of depression, Jess had thought, Chris had told Dave and Dave's sister, Kat, the previous Saturday at Henderson Park, that he would only go to the LDS Valentine's Day romp if the little Catholic girl came with the rest of the gang.

Dave had passed the news to Tam.

Tam somehow got the boulder rolling. But even after the dance, that big round rock seemed to get stuck tonight.

Now, everyone was gone but the two girls, sitting in the cab of a truck under a thundering rain.

Blinking at the sun visor, Tam slowed her weeping. "I guess I was lying to myself."

"What do you mean?" said Jess, a little nervous. The past four weeks, Tam had been nothing but a beacon of hope and happy dreams.

"Maybe Chris didn't want you to—"

Jess reeled back a bit and cut her off. "Didn't want me?"

Sniveling, Tam searched in her purse for tissues. "Well, not at first, anyway." She sniffed extra loud with her nose aimed at her bag. With the back of her wrist, she brushed tears from her right eye. Tam showed Jess her teeth in a false smile, enunciating her words with almost sarcastic precision. "But you have that magnetic personality!"

Moaning and growling, Jess massaged her forehead. Her long dusty-blonde hair—the blonde being the added part of what she grew up thinking 'boring'—continued to drip rainwater. She wanted to go outside and give it a good wringing, but that wouldn't work.

Magnetic personality, huh? "Only *you* think so, Tam."

"Well I know Ryan Stokes would agree with me."

"Let's not visit ex-boyfriends tonight, okay?"

Weeping again, Tam picked up her purse and slammed it into her thighs. "*Why* can't I *find* anything in *here*?!"

Something else was wrong, but Tam wasn't telling. Jess knew her, though. They'd been friends for life.

I'm not going to push it, Jess decided.

"We should get out of here."

Jess fiddled with Dave's keys. She slid away a house key, another, a key to Dave's mother's Honda, then stopped on a small cylinder of silver metal.

"It's just," Tam looked up again, brushing her eyes with her fingertips, "you and Chris ... I *saw* you. At the dance, in the foyer, hiding in the halls, even when there was nowhere else left to hide and I found you and I pushed you both onto the floor at the beginning of that slow dance. Oh, girl! *I know* what I saw in your eyes. And I know what I saw in his."

"You didn't see Chris leave at the end of the day." Jess slid her fingers over the short metal post she had found on the key ring. *What was this?*

"Yes I *did*."

Jess shook her head. She kept her eyes on her hands in the shadows under the steering wheel. "He was running away. Once outside, he couldn't even look at me."

"I remember you laughing together in the church." Tam chuckled. "You had his *watch*, didn't you? And you wouldn't give it back."

Jess couldn't suppress the smile. Tears clouded her vision. "Yes."

"He'd reach for it. You'd jerk away. Then you'd hold it out like bait. You are such a flirt! And you wouldn't return it when it became obvious that he meant to snag it out of your grasp at all cost."

Jess laughed. Tears exploded from her eyes so hard, she had to reach up to catch them and hold them out of sight. *The Valentine's dance … it had been such a wonderful night.* "I had to clamp his watch with both hands, once he started to wrestle with me—I couldn't *believe* it was happening!"

"You *wanted* it, girl!" Tam nudged her with an elbow and wiped away the wetness from her eyes again. "You turned your back to him. You *forced* him to reach around you to get that watch."

"I held it to my gut and bent over—"

"But you never ran away!" Tam laughed with her friend and cried with her at the same time.

"Even though Chris kept coming."

"You let him reach around left, reach around right. Then he wrapped you with both of those big arms. Such a muscle man!"

"Oh, Tamara."

"And you just snuggled into him, giggling the whole

time, saying, 'No sir, this watch is my *payment* for coming to this pagan dance in the first place!'"

The girls embraced, spilling tears and laughing without shame.

Tam sniffed again. "And Chris didn't once fight that watch away from you. Not until Sister Fowler showed up and scolded all of us toward the dance floor."

"That woman was freaky," said Jess.

"Trust you me, I know her! She would have walked us to the middle of the floor and stood there, holding a *Book of Mormon* between your tummies as you danced, if that car alarm hadn't gone off right outside where those other boys were taping red hearts all over the doors and windows."

"I still didn't give Chris his watch back." Jess struggled to dispel the grin on her face and close her eyes, while she dreamed her way back to those breathtaking moments.

She had gotten so busted by her Dad later.

And she hadn't cared at all.

"Then when the dance was nearly over, I shoved the two of you into the music and dimmed lights myself." Tam swallowed, turning her own eyes up and back to that fabulous evening. "He got his watch … He was holding you. *Chris Noble*! The last boy to leave Rita Hirsch's powerful wake. You know, I hear she still wants him?"

Her voice far off in memory now, Jess said, "What song did Chris and I dance to, Tam?"

"What's that?"

Jess shrugged. "I recognized most of what the DJ played at the dance. But I'd never heard that song—so beautiful. I don't remember any of the words. I'm not even sure I heard them. And I've ... listened around for our song since."

"*Our* song?" Tam chuckled.

"Even jumped from station to station trying to hear it again. I'd recognize the tune."

"No, girl. That's one song you won't hear on the radio in Harmon, California. At least not until the Millennium, I figure."

"I keep meaning to google it. You know who was it? Kind of sounded like ... Sting, or the Police." With eyes glazed, Jess noticed she was rocking a bit. Steeling herself, she cleared her throat. "A slow song."

"Sting!" said Tam, laughing harder. "I thought the same thing too, in middle school. Nope. Brett Raymond—really cool."

"And—"

"And the song you and tall-dark-and-handsome Chris danced to is called—are you ready?"

"I've *been* ready, Tam!" Jess leveled her gaze.

"'I Need Thee Every Hour.' *Nobody* but Brett Raymond could sing that song in a way to inspire a DJ to play it at an LDS dance."

"That's it!" Jess barked a single laugh. "I've been *so hungry* to remember." She shut her eyes and sang the few bars that came to mind. "I need thee ... oh, I *need* thee ...

every hour ... oh, I need thee ... ." She opened her eyes. "*So* romantic, Tam."

Sniggering a little more, Tam cocked her head toward her friend. "Well girl, that's not *exactly*, how it goes. And it's a church *hymn*."

"Who cares," said Jess, as a wave of cold shivered down her arms to the strange key ring in her hands. She took a deep breath and stared out the window. "I will love that song for the rest of my life."

Still laughing, Tam said, "I hope so!" She relaxed with a hum, then peered at the devastation she had caused inside her purse. "Ah, man."

With a groan and then a frown, Jess shut her eyes. "But then he left me, Tam. Chris went home with Dave." She looked at the peculiar object in her hands again. "He went down the steps ... said, 'See ya.' Didn't even look back."

"Yeah, while you stood there at the glass like a girl who just got her Barbie stolen. And *then* you started asking about Ben, as if nothing magical had just lit up your life—*Ben!*" Tam laughed, less sincere this time and more sarcastic. Her voice reclaimed a pinch of seriousness. "The only Mormon boy who would *never* show up at a church function like that."

"Well, I feel safe around my cousin, okay?" Jess wiped her eyes and nose again. "Even though he's a member of your church; Ben never makes me feel like I'm the target of some fellowshipping effort, or that I'm not righteous enough to be privy to your little Mormon secrets."

"Jess!" Tam squinted at her. "You've hung around with Mormon kids for years. You never told me you felt that way. And I certainly never tried to turn you into some kind of third wheel."

"Yeah, well, okay. What's this, then." Jess lifted the keys into the light, which shimmered, splitting colors through the rainwater pounding and sliding down the windshield.

"That?" Tam swallowed.

"What are these words cut into the metal?" Jess brought them closer to her eyes, blinked, concentrated until she could make out the tiny letters:

HOLD TO THE ROD

"Oh," Tam only glanced at the thin cylinder. "Ah, just a little kid thing in our church."

"Why are you lying to me?"

Jess tried to twist the object, pull it into two parts as Chris had done in the glow of hot white light under their orange and black umbrella in the rain.

No matter how hard she pulled and strained, the silver rod remained whole.

She looked at it again. In the dim and flickering light— blue and yellow from the overhead BURGER sign, pink from the red flares on the road, orange-yellow flashing from the tow truck parked almost right in the middle of Sunrise

Boulevard, and red and blue from bursts atop the cop cars—Jess couldn't see where the metal tube would open.

And it sure seemed too thin to hold anything.

Chris had said the word *Oil*. What did he mean?

Tam lowered her brow. "I don't lie to my friends, Jess. Especially best friends. And I don't hurt them with sharp accusations, either."

Oh yeah? thought Jess. *Wasn't that a sharp accusation?*

Folding her arms, Tam lifted her chin. "I think I want to go home now."

"Sorry." Jess put the key in the ignition and started the engine like someone who had never driven before. She removed her foot from the gas pedal and the high-pitched wail under the hood unwound to a steady hum.

In the rearview mirror, Jess noticed the cops turning to stare at her.

Tam shut her purse with a snap. "Just tell me one thing."

Jess said nothing and didn't meet Tamara's eyes as she pulled out of the parking lot.

When they stopped at a red light and Tam waited too long for her to bear, Jess moaned. "All right, what."

"Do you love him?"

Jess thought of the truth. Then she said, "No."

Tam blinked once, nodded once. Nodded again. "Okay, girl."

The light turned green.

Jess floored it.

Chapter Four

"You sure you don't want us to take you home, Dave?" said Chris's father in the front seat of the Buick. He would have been deemed a handsome man had he not lost his left eyebrow in a bicycle accident at the age of sixteen. "It's past midnight."

"Thanks, Brother Noble. But I have to get my truck."

Chris's mother, a beautiful woman with a full head of prematurely white hair, turned to look into the back seat. "Your mother called our house. We didn't know where you were at the time. I thought you should know."

Dave nodded with a stale grin. "Turn at the next light."

Leaning close, Chris said, "You want to spend the night?"

"No can do," said Dave. "Not anymore."

"School night?"

"Weekends only." Dave kept his voice beneath the drone of Josh Groban playing up front. "As I get older, my Mom thinks I'm turning into my Dad."

They stared at each other for a moment. "Are you?"

"Gosh, I hope not." Running a hand through his trashed hair, Dave nudged Chris with an elbow. "What are you going to tell Jess?"

Chris looked at the ceiling. "I don't know what I'm doing anymore, Dave. I shouldn't have gone out with her tonight."

"You didn't want to?"

Scratching his neck, Chris glanced out the window at the silent storm clouds lit by yellow city lights. "I never said that."

Dave shifted in his seat. "Well, missionary boy, you could always convert her."

Chris studied the rearview mirror to watch for the eyes of his inquisitive father. "That might only make things worse."

"Doesn't in the storybooks."

"And which books would those be?"

"I meant the movies." Dave shifted again. "You know, church videos. It's the only good part about going to seminary." He lifted his voice. "Right at the top of the hill, Brother Noble."

With a playfully southern drawl, Chris's father said, "Yooou got it!"

Chris watched his mother's head rock back and forth as the car swayed and rolled over bumps in the road. He couldn't tell if she was asleep or listening intently to the clandestine words of the boys in back.

"I'm beginning to wish I'd paid more attention to my

seminary teachers."

Dave sneered. "What are you talking about, *Peter*." Whenever Chris did something overtly righteous, Dave called him that, which was short for Peter Priesthood, of course. "You never missed a day, remember."

"I shouldn't have said that. It's a lie. I've got to learn to stop lying."

"I know. My sophomore year, before I could drive, I was supposed to catch a ride with you. When you didn't show up, Sister Hirsch took me, remember?"

"Oh yeah."

Dave clapped a hand onto his friend's shoulder. "And you may also recall, my friend, that was in the days of Rita's braces."

Chris stared at the clouds again. He knew Dave was insulting the young woman. Chris had fallen for her anyway. Later, they'd gotten together. She swam in a pool, her long black hair trailing over her white one piece. Chris still remembered how he felt that day, looking at her. And he hated himself for those feelings. He wished he could have risen above them. In time, and in his own way, he had. Now Rita was history.

The braces hadn't mattered at all.

Spitting on the picture of Chris's ex-girlfriend was Dave's way of making Chris feel better.

"What did you *not* learn in seminary?"

Chris looked him in the eye. "Everything." He looked at the seat. "Nothing." He looked out the window. "I remember stories. I read bits of scripture here and there. I memorized most of the Scripture Mastery verses as part of assignments."

Dave poked him. "You learned a lot."

"I guess I did. My heart just wasn't in it, I suppose."

"Not like now?"

Chris waited for a moment, then nodded.

"Do you love her?"

All the liquid evaporated from Chris's throat. "Jessica?"

Dave leaned forward. "The brown house with the dying pine trees, Brother Noble. That's my truck out front."

They pulled up in front of the home of Jessica Singer.

A bedroom light glowed from one window on the far side.

Chris cleared his throat, then met eyes with Dave after he opened the door and stepped out. He couldn't say anything. He didn't dare.

Dave pressed his lips together. "Thanks Brother Noble, Sister Noble. Call you tomorrow, Chris."

"Right," said Chris.

On the way home, his mother said only one thing: "You went out with that Catholic girl again?"

Chapter Five

The lunch bell might as well have been a fire alarm for a pack of loonies doing their best to look cool. Students exploded from classroom doors. Like ants they rushed in every direction, and the din of chitchat reached a throbbing volume almost instantly. Names were shouted. Girls screamed. Everybody laughed.

Tamara saw Dave come out of the men's locker room with only a backpack slung over his shoulder. When slammed by the wind, his brown hair lifted into spikes and did a little dance.

Since the end of the cross-country season his junior year, Dave wore the telltale blue and gold letterman's jacket. Running represented the only sports achievement he had contributed to Harmon High's athletic program.

All the coaches, and even the school counselor—a bald man Dave visited with regularity—had urged him to play football because of his impressive height and muscular weight.

He hadn't told any of the grownups that his father had been a fullback. And he had sworn all the guys, who knew the truth, to secrecy, under penalty of death.

Dave hated his dad for leaving him, Katrina, and their pregnant mother for some other woman.

The trama of divorce had been too severe. Dave's mom had lost the baby.

Whether just or unjust, Dave blamed his dad for that too.

So he never played football, ever.

When he saw Tamara running over to him, Dave lowered his head and started walking a little faster.

"Dave, I don't think I can do this." Matching his pace, and having to skip sometimes to do so, Tam held her hands in front of her as she spoke. "Jess is starting to ask questions."

"So?"

"After what happened last night, she's not going to stop."

"So let her ask." Dave crossed the quad toward his locker.

"Easy for you to say. *I'm* her best friend. She knows we're hiding something. *I'm* not comfortable with this agreement! She'll expect me to give it up." Tam glanced over the faces scrambling by, hastening into the lunch hour. She didn't see Jessica—that was the important thing. "Dave?"

He gazed about as if he hadn't heard her.

"Why don't we tell her?"

"She doesn't need to know, okay?" he said, speeding his

step.

"Yeah, 'cept in front of the burger shop—"

"Hey! I didn't plan the accident. Go blame the elders for not watching the road."

Grabbing the leather sleeve of his jacket, she tugged to make him stop. "*You guys* didn't have to save them!"

"We *didn't*?" He pushed his face into hers and tightened his grip on his backpack. "What were we supposed to do, let a missionary drown?!? *There's* a way to get points in heaven! If we didn't get excommunicated, angels would probably assassinate us in our sleep!"

Tam laughed. Both consequences were ludicrous. "You don't believe that."

Not intending it to be a joke, he jerked away from her.

Catching up and skipping a bit to keep pace with his massive legs, Tam rubbed her hands through her red hair. "Dave—"

"Look." He spun on her again and poked a finger into her face. "Last night was *your* idea, remember. It was a bad plan. You should have known better."

"Me? What about you! You said they looked good together! You wanted to come!"

He tilted his head and gave a grin that was really a grimace. "You promised you'd buy me a hamburger. I know Chris better than anyone. Not only *wouldn't* he recognize it as a date, but he wouldn't let anything romantic happen between him and Jess anyway."

"Why not?"

He blinked and stared around him as if he were the only sane man alive. "She's a Catholic, Tam. He's a Mormon. Do the addition any way you want. The sum is always *zero*."

Rounding a corner and driving a hole through the crowds racing for lunch lines, Dave slowed his pace.

Tam folded her arms, her face radiating heat so much, she knew it was red. "Well, I think I should tell her then."

That stopped him. He snapped to attention, grabbed her arm, then sagged forward enough to rub noses with her if he'd tried. "You are Jess's best friend, Tam. Look me in the eye and tell me the news won't rip out her heart."

Tam bit her tongue between her molars, shifting her jawbone to the right. Her eyes fluttered against the pressure of tears. She wasn't going to cry in front of Dave. No way. "At least Jess would have a fighting chance."

Dave grinned, though his brown eyes darkened as he let his backpack drop to his side. It hung from the tips of his fingers as if weightless. "Did you hear what you just said, Tam? Do you have any idea how bad that sounds? Remember the story of the three devils you tried to tell us last night?"

"You calling me a devil?" Her voice cracked.

He sighed hard enough to cause him to clear his throat. "Tam. You do what you have to do. Frankly, I thought you were above this."

"Because, unlike yourself, I'm loyal to my best friend? What about Chris's feelings?" She had to wipe away the wetness in her eyes, and that only made things more un-nerving.

No boy thinks a weeping woman is beautiful, she told herself.

Dave certainly wouldn't.

Taking a step away, he shook his head. "I told Chris after Valentine's Day he needed to tell Jessica, straight up, to—"

Tam put her hands on her hips. "To what."

Dave took another step away, closer to his locker, though he leaned forward as he spoke.

Strangers passed between them.

Their eyes didn't disconnect.

"To go away."

"But … " Tam's voice clogged. Moisture escaped her eyelids and trickled down her right cheek.

Slinging the backpack over his shoulder again, Dave raised empty hands into the air and opened his eyes wide. "But? What, Tamara?"

The tear dropped off her chin. "Chris loves her."

Grinding his teeth, Dave hooked a thumb under the strap of his backpack and started walking backward again toward the wall of baby-blue lockers. "Go eat lunch."

She nodded, furious, needing to visit the lady's room, and wondering what had ever attracted her to this super-sized ex-runner. He didn't even go to seminary every day. "Fine."

Grabbing the dial of the locker beside his own, Dave

spun out his combination. "And Tam?"

"What."

Dave gave her a flat smile. "When Kat finds out that you're telling Jess, don't plan on using me as a human shield."

She grinned as he pulled up on the lock to find the locker wasn't his.

As she turned away, he punched his fist into the blue sheet metal.

Chapter Six

"What. Are you sitting all by yourself today?"

Jess rested her chin on her right shoulder to see her lanky cousin, Ben Wainwright, swing his legs over the wooden bench and plop down. Squinting in the high-noon light, she searched the settling crowds up the grass hill and over on the pink-top of the quad. "Guess so."

The majority of the students in the school, who used this period for lunch, had taken up their typical positions or were slowly arriving there: jocks, cheerleaders, and popular mean girls dominated the quad; stoners claimed the wall behind the band building; the drama kings and queens filled the cafeteria; Latinos took over the concrete walkway that led to the academic classes and lockers; and the sloping school green made room for the more peaceful sort—or at least, that was Jess's observation.

"Well I don't think you smell too bad." Ben rolled two crushed tuna sandwiches out of a brown paper sack. "I'll eat with ya."

"You always eat with us."

"Yep. Though *us* isn't the word I'd use today. What

did you do, make fun of Tamara's older brother and his big-old-rabbit thumb-sucking teeth again?" Curling both hands beside his mouth, he sucked in his bottom lip, shoved out his incisors, then made high-pitched squeaking noises.

Offering a smile as a sign of amity, Jessica said, "That would be the voice of a squirrel, my friend."

He shrugged. "Same thing. If you got 'em, flaunt 'em. Isn't that right? Oh, no!" He reached into the bottom of his bag and removed a piece of wax paper. Attached to this little sheet *and* to the bottom of the bag, he pulled what looked like a string of red gum. Lifting his hand higher and higher, the line of goo extended. Ben dropped the bag into the grass and looked at his fingers, which had not yet been slimed. Then he stood, slowly, stretching the red line from the bottom of the bag and into the sky. When it still didn't break, he stood on the bench and carried the pinch of wax paper towards the heaven.

"Don't let me fall," he said.

Jess grimaced and forced down a swell of laughter trying to escape her throat. "What *is* that?!" It couldn't be gum.

The thin red line refused to snap.

"Um." Ben looked around. "Could you hand me one of those sandwiches?"

"I don't know which would be worse to touch, Ben." With one fingernail, she scratched at a blob comprised of cellophane wrapped around bread that had squished into the shape of a roll of oozing tuna and mayonnaise.

"Trust me." Ben waved the red line in her direction. "You'd never get this out of your hair. Or off your clothes."

She screamed as the line wiggled toward her in the air, and *still* didn't break. "Okay-okay!" She gave him the sandwich.

Like a ninja from the famed—but *possibly* never existing—Todai Cooking School of Death, Ben gave a Karate shriek and hacked his tuna blade through the endlessly dripping line of ooze.

The sugar snake, cut in two, dropped, writhing through the air, and lay dead in the grass to be devoured by birds or squirrels or other small-brained creatures.

"Gross!"

"Ha, ha!" Ben plopped onto the bench. He lifted the squirming red string high above his head and lowered the end of it toward his mouth. Though the end of the candy caught on his upper lip, he was able to feed the rest of it down into his gullet to digest, perhaps, in a few hours.

"That's disgusting." Jess let the laugh escape for a second.

"Homemade cinnamon taffy. Just like mamma makes!" he said over the twists and rolls of red tangling inside his mouth.

"Who made it?"

"My mom. Great stuff! Though I'd prefer she wrap it a little better, or at least give me some heads-up that it's in there so I don't go and let it melt all over the bottom of my lunch bag. Look how much I wasted!"

She pointed. "It's still there, Ben. Go ahead! Pork it out of there. I won't tell anyone."

He smirked at her.

She showed her upper teeth and squeaked at him.

"So where's Tam, then?"

Her face darkened in a hurry. "Ah, I haven't talked to her since last night."

"Bummer of an evening? Not the Big Date everyone hoped for?" he said, tying a shoelace that had run free during his altercation with dessert.

"It wasn't a date, Benjamin."

"Ouch," he said. "That bad, huh?"

"I didn't say that."

"Yeah, but you called me Benjamin. Always a bad sign. You're not eating?"

She gazed upon the bench beside her, at the plastic tray of fruit, raisin bran, and chocolate milk she'd picked up in the cafeteria.

He examined it as well, humming. "Yum. Your regular health store for body builders, yes sir."

Drawing her heels up the edge of the bench and wrapping her arms around her knees, she watched the American flag flapping against the puffy cotton that dotted the sky. "It was a bad idea to go last night. I don't know what I was thinking."

Nodding while he ate, Ben's head slowed as his eyes searched hers.

She felt his patient stare like a warm sun on her cheek. If he didn't look away soon, she was liable to lose it. At the same time, she couldn't think of a single distraction to use to change the subject.

Her cousin took a bite of tuna, its strong odor wafting under her nose. He waited forever, then swallowed and looked at the mile-long worm he had left in the grass. "Wasn't interested?"

He didn't look up; he kept things safe for her. Ben was always good at playing things safe. And just in time too, for a single tear dribbled down the side of her nose, the side he would see if he stared again. So much moisture gathered in the back of her throat, that when Jess spoke, the words came out a gurgle of pain: "He didn't want me."

She put one hand over her eyes as if for shade and leaned her head forward. Tears released from her lashes and splashed onto the blades of green at her feet. She hoped no one would see her and come over, especially when her shoulders began to bob as she heaved and wept as silently as possible.

"All right, cuz'." An old pal, Ben kept his chin high and his eyes averted. He wrapped one arm around her shoulders, his hand in an unromantic fist as he gave her one squeeze and then another.

Jess hadn't cried after dropping Tam off last night. She hadn't shed a tear when she heard Dave knocking on her bedroom window after midnight, nor when she had asked him how things had gone at the hospital with the missionary who'd gotten hurt, nor when Dave had given a shrug and a nod and only said one word: "Keys?" And she hadn't cried when Dave had taken them from her hand, climbed into his truck, and driven away into what had become by then only a memory of a storm.

"So Tam's not mad about it, is she?" said Ben.

"No. I think she was embarrassed by the whole thing."

Ben laughed. "Tamara Cline? That girl *can't* get embarrassed. She's in drama!" He leaned close to Jess's ear. "Drama ... every day of her multicolored life, take my word for it. She only becomes a normal person on the stage, and *only* when it's a mystery or a tragedy. Did you see her kiss Bobby Blackum in *We Honor the Gentlemen*? Now *that* was real! I was jealous, and I'm not even in love with her!"

With the tears wiped away, Jess smiled kindly and let his arm fall. She ripped the plastic off her fruit and spooned pineapple, pear, and cherry into her mouth like a starving woman after a long walk in the desert. "I didn't see Tam at our locker this morning."

"She sick today?"

"No." Jess fiddled with her lunch. "She was in biology, but the teacher had her dissecting giant worms with her group; they're a little behind the rest of the class because Paul Meyer and his twin brother thought they had mono and didn't show all this week."

"Tam's in a group with two twins in the same class? That must get confusing."

"Don't you remember? She told you all about them." Jess squinted at her cousin and slowed her speech. "But I think at the word *Twins*, you started daydreaming about those Wilkins girls."

He smiled with the left side of his face. "Probably. I never listen to anything important. It's kind of a goal in life."

"Well, we didn't get to talk. Tam stayed busy, and I …I guess I haven't been able to concentrate on my classes much. She *did* have that secretive look about her though, like she was keeping something from me though part of her wanted to tell."

Ben hummed in thought, then chewed along.

Jess shook her head. "What is it with you Mormons and your secrets anyway?"

He tossed his shoulders and took another bite, watching a clique of pretty girls follow the sidewalk up the grass hill. "I don't know."

"Well … don't you go to seminary?"

"Are you really asking me this? My Catholic cousin, who goes to mass every Saturday night without fail, just to please her dying father, who probably hasn't gone himself in ten years?" He chuckled. "What do you care about *religion*, Jess?"

"You *don't* go to seminary?"

"Young lady, I go every single morning. I'm there at six sharp, rain or shine, even when the sun's still hiding behind the mountains. I have no choice!"

"So what are all these secret passwords and Chinese locks?"

He laughed again. "I have no idea."

"Well what do you do at seminary, sleep?!?"

Leaning close again, Ben said, "Every single morning of the school year!" He stuck out his red-dyed tongue and laughed tuna breath.

Jess recoiled against both sight and smell. "Well, Dave only goes half the time, I understand. They really let you do that? Sleep?"

He nodded with pride. "In my pajamas, no less! But I have to sit in a desk. And I get A's, too, because all those sweet-hearted teachers are afraid of hurting my self-esteem and driving me into inactivity."

"What's that?"

"No more Peter Priesthood." He laughed again.

It was a mocking laugh, though Jess knew he wasn't assaulting her. She spread a hand between them. "Well that's what I'm talking about. A Mormon codeword at every turn. Sly glances. Evil laughs. Do you guys think it's supposed to amuse me or something?"

Raising both hands in defense, Ben said, "Whoa-whoa."

Jess hadn't stopped talking. "I thought I was going out of my mind at Blaine's Burger. Everyone telling Mormon jokes and Mormon stories. All eyes darting out the window like they could *feel* the missionaries drawing near. Even before the accident, Tam tried diverting my attention by—"

"Accident?! Wait-wait-wait. Accident?" He shook his hands and blinked his eyes and squinted at her, tilting his head to the right.

She stood, faced him, and shut her eyes. "Just tell me one thing. What do you Mormons put inside of a container that bears the words Hold To The Rod?"

When she opened her eyes, Ben's mouth hung slightly ajar. One eyebrow remained level while the other bent low.

Ben shook his head. He flopped his hands up, fingers splayed, and then down to his lap. "Can't help you."

Folding her arms, Jess cocked her hip to the side and licked her bottom teeth. "Can't? Or won't?"

He rolled his head to the right, keeping his eyeball aimed at her face. "Jess—"

"Forget it." Jess spun away. "Just, never mind."

"Come on, cuz'," he said on his feet as she pounded through the grass. "Come back here."

Raising her voice, she said, "I thought you were different, Benjamin. I thought I could *talk* to you."

"Then let's talk!" he yelled.

"Jess?" said another voice.

She froze and looked up. Chris?

No. Why did she think it was him, come to bar her way and explain all the Mormon mysteries, maybe even take her hand and lead her away from this miserable planet?

Ryan Stokes, her ex-boyfriend, stood in her path.

"Oh, no."

Chapter Seven

"You know what will happen if you hang out with those pot-heads."

Dave had almost made it out of sight for lunch. The last person he wanted to eat with right now was any member of the LDS church. He stopped, shut his eyes, and aimed them at the sky.

Great, he thought. *Just the person I hoped to avoid most.*

With arms folded and a scowl fighting to cover the worry in her eyes, Katrina Martinez, his beloved sister, waited for him to respond. Kat was the kind of girl who would be strikingly beautiful, if she wasn't your sister. Most guys considered her perfect cheerleader material, visually speaking—it was her "personal dating code" that caused them to suffer.

"You following me? Are Molly Mormons allowed to engage in covert operations?"

"I know you too well, David. When you picked me up from seminary this morning and didn't say a word, I told myself, My brother doesn't want to talk to me about last night—and that means something bad happened. I heard

Mom attack you when you got home after midnight."

"So what," said Dave. He checked his watch and sighed to let her know the lunch hour was quickly slipping away. "Look I—"

"Just tell me one thing, David. Is it starting? Does Jess know?"

"That's two things, Kat. I gotta go eat, okay?"

"With your old smoking buddies?" She shook her head. "They're only going to devil-whisper in your ear, you know." Strangling her voice a bit, in imitation of the stoners, she said, "Hey, man. You don't look so good. Try this! It'll make everything better, I promise. And I won't tell your fascist Mormon sister nothing."

Dave looked across the pink-painted asphalt to the bench on the grass where he sometimes sat with Jess, Tam, Ben, and a few other guys and gals from seminary. For all the cheerleaders and swimmers parked in the way around a large tree with enormous maple leaves, he couldn't see anyone over there. Had everyone abandoned Jess?

"What would Chris say if he knew you'd gone back to hanging out with those losers from your sophomore year?"

"Who cares." Dave started to walk away.

"Oh!" she said, raising her eyebrows. "So you don't mind if I let that info slip the next time he comes over? I don't know, but a young man going through the changes Chris is making in his life right now is liable to go find a *new* best friend."

Flipping around, he stabbed a finger at her. "If he's

so bulletproof, why are you panicked about Jess getting involved?"

"People *fall*, Dave. Put the best girl and best guy together in the wrong situation, and they drop—haven't you learned anything from seminary?"

"Is that why you don't have a boyfriend, Kat?"

Katrina recoiled.

"Is that why you've *never* had a boyfriend? Or is it because you are so good, so obedient, or because you have such a *sweet spirit* and nothing else to go with it?"

Kat hugged her books to her chest. She turned and started walking away.

Dave kicked the toe of one shoe into the brick corner of the building.

He shouldn't have said that, and he knew it. He didn't get along with his mother, mostly because he had no memory of her getting along with his father before the divorce. In fact, he had heard the word "divorce" so many times when he was small that he and his sister had come to call it the forbidden D Word.

Kat was all that Dave really had in the way of family.

Somehow, she rose above darkness while he bounced like a buoy out at sea: sometimes up and in the light, other times drowning in green and murky waters. "Kat…"

She turned, slow and red-eyed. "That was mean, Dave."

"I know," said Dave, which was always his sincerest way of apologizing.

"You're above that sort of talk," she said.

He lifted his chin and grit his teeth. "Am I?"

He wanted to be. Sometimes, as the child of an emotionally abusive father, he wondered if he would not someday become the same sort of man: "The curse of the fathers answered on the heads of the children to the third and fourth generation," his seminary teacher had once said. That sort of thing.

Kat shook her scowl. "Chris Noble wouldn't have insulted a sister—or anyone for that matter—in the way you have hurt me."

Leaning into the wind, Dave squinted and raised his voice. "Well if you haven't noticed, Kat, *I am not Chris Noble!*"

He stormed away, around the side of the building.

Yep, he thought. The words were different, but that conversation sure sounded the same as the kind he had heard at night while trying to sleep, the kind he had always heard down the hallway, while he tried to say prayers at the side of the bed, praying, hoping that someday his mother and father would love each other, that they might become a good LDS family, the kind he heard about at church. They were prayers that he had not seen answered.

Yeah. Maybe I am becoming my father. Wherever he is.

Does that also means my Molly Mormon sister will become the other half.

In the end, he determined, *we will all be spiritually dead—if we don't pull out of this dive.*

He hi-fived his smoking buddies as he passed them.

One growled over a twist of marijuana. "Not eating with us today?"

Dave shook his head and kept walking. "Need to be alone, boys."

"It's cool. You come around when you want. We'll keep the wall warm for you."

Dave went into the baseball field and sat on third.

Instead of eating, he looked at the sky for a very long time.

Chapter Eight

"Please go away Ryan," said Jess as he stepped in her path.

She moved left.

He stayed with her.

She shifted to the right, and he matched her footing again. She sighed from her gut. "I'm through dancing with you."

"Jess, what are you afraid of?" He tugged at the cuffs of a letterman's jacket covered in golden pins. "Think I'm going to kiss you with ol' Mormon boy ready to run over here and sacrifice his life in your defense? Don't worry. I'm not in the mood for killing skinny weaklings today."

Jess showed him the palm of her hand. "I'm not talking to you."

She eased left.

He jumped in her way again, glancing over her shoulder at Ben Wainwright. "Why not?"

She had to look.

Ben didn't rise at all. He watched without blinking, and he chomped and chewed. Some hero, Jess said to herself.

"Jess …." Ryan moved a little to let her walk. When she passed him, he added, "You and I have more of a relationship than you've got with Chris Noble."

Laughing, Jess said, "Ryan, *we* have *no relationship* anymore. What do you think you know about Chris anyway?"

"Same as everyone else at Harmon High, by now. Tamara's been blowing her non-stop bullhorn in class all morning."

Jess rubbed both eyes with one hand.

"Oh, yeah!" said Ryan, now that he had hooked her. "Said there was a big accident in front of Blaine's Burger. Some bystander got cleaned right off the road by a yellow Chevy."

Nodding with a serious face as if this was the first she had heard of it, Jess folded her arms.

"But you know all about it, don't you." Ryan leaned close. "You were there on a date with Chris."

She opened her mouth to lie.

He spoke too fast for her. "And he wasn't interested."

Another punch in the stomach. Jess flinched at the truth of his words. When she remembered to draw breath, she cleared her throat to speak. Tears came out of her face instead.

Using sheer willpower, she dried them before they could run down her cheeks. Her face, however, Jess could not cool. Her coloring no doubt revealed her emotions.

"I'm sorry." Ryan's eyes bounced to the grass and back

into her eyes.

She started at the sidewalk. "Yeah." She laughed. "Sure."

He grabbed her arm, putting the brakes on their pace. "No, Jess. Really. *I* care. Or is that something you forgot when you humiliated me in front of half my team at the Winter Ball."

"Some people just can't take 'Get the heck off me' for an answer, I guess." Her voice cracked as she chilled the heat blooms in her face with steady breathing.

With hands stuffed into the pockets of his jeans, he swiveled and spoke while peering in every direction. "If you're going to play hard to get with me again, I can respect that."

"Ha!"

"But remember at least that I am Catholic like you— something I can't say about the crowd you're hanging with more and more." He grinned. "They're going to try to convert you, you know."

"So?" she said, calm again, or at least as relaxed as she had managed to be all day: an outward peace while earthquakes broke every five seconds under her skin.

He tapped his chest. "I know your father only has you left." He smiled at the grass. "He was so happy when we'd go to mass together on Saturday nights."

"Even though he never went," she said. It was a point of bitterness Jessica often revealed to others, though she would never share those hurt feelings with her dad. He so wanted to know that she took communion. He would ask her every week about the sermon.

"You're a good daughter. I mean, he's so old ... When he made you promise to go every Saturday night, I figured you'd toss it in his face. Or at least try to get out of it. Or if not that, ditch and *say* you went."

"I couldn't do that to my father." Her voice cracked again. Surprised, her eyes opened wide. She swallowed the pain away and moseyed onto the cement walk.

"Well, that's what I'm saying. A good Catholic girl like you who's promised her old man she'll go to church, no matter what ... and a Mormon crowd who would pull you away from that? 'Get thee to a nunnery!'"

She looked into a bush and concentrated on the green leaves and the bittersweet odor rising from them so she wouldn't start to weep and fall into Ryan's waiting arms.

Ryan always had such a powerful voice. He knew what to say to make her do what he wanted. Manipulation was one of the reasons she had broken it off. "Jess. The *idea* that you and Chris might hit it off ... is flawed from the beginning."

She shook her head.

Oh, Chris! she thought, and the urge to fall into Ryan's embrace overwhelmed her. She needed those arms around her—if not Chris's arms. She needed to smell the cologne of a young man up close. And Ryan might do if Chris didn't care for her. She ached for the warm squeeze of Chris's hug, and for his chin on the top of her head, and the sound of his breathing as her ear pressed against his neck.

Had that happened at the Valentine's Day dance? She'd seen that touch and burn in his magic blue eyes. Chris had wanted to be close as much as she did …or had those been her thoughts, her sensations, her memories transposed onto the experience as she replayed it?

"Ryan." Jess shook her head to the side to ease the pressure. "Do you … have a stick of gum. I *must* have the breath of a dissected frog, after the fruit I ate today.

He didn't say anything. A young man who had practiced the move a hundred times, Ryan slid his fingers into the left pocket of his letterman's jacket and came out, not only with his yellow pack of Juicy Fruit, but with one stick protruding an inch and a half from his fist.

After putting the gum into her mouth and handing back the empty wrapper—which Ryan held to his lips and nose and sniffed once slowly—Jess said, "Why does it seem like the entire planet is talking about religion these days?"

"Well," he said to the sky, sliding his left hand back into his jeans again, "if you ask your Latter-day friends, they'll say it's the end of the world."

"And you?" Jess gave him a friendly smile. No, that hadn't been friendly, she realized. That was a *flirtatious* smile, the sort she had shown him many times. Before.

Why did I do that? she thought. *Am I a girl so lonely that on the rebound I would go to my ex-boyfriend for comfort? Aargh!*

"Me? I'm just happy to be able to talk to you."

She nodded, something polite, something less suggestive—*Can't I even control myself?* she wondered.

"What. Can't handle your Mormon friends and their secrets anymore?"

Jess looked into his face and drew close enough to whisper. "I just can't understand why Tam and the others won't share with me, some of the time."

"Want to know?" With a smile and a lick of lips, Ryan glanced around to make sure no one else would hear this precious bit of knowledge. "After Kat Martinez came onto me—"

"No, Ryan. Kat blew *you* off when you started with the lines and the 'Hey babe' moves, remember? *Everybody* knows that."

"Yeah-whatever," he said with his eyes shut. "Anyway, Anthony Wilde—remember him? My second-class halfback?"

Jess peered across the grass to her bench. Ben Wainwright was still there, munching his tuna rolls and giving her a shake of the head to let her know that talking with an ex-beau is always a bad idea. She knew he was right. "Go on," she said anyway.

"Well he's one of these I've-said-two-words-and-now-I'm-saved kind of Protestant Christians." Ryan shimmied his hands in the air, then flopped them to his sides. "Still, a good friend of mine."

"So what," she said, hoofing toward the arch where the

quad gave way to classrooms and the endless walls of baby-blue lockers. Why had she even *thought* for a moment that going back to Ryan might be a good idea? Repulsive!

"Well, Anthony gave me this little booklet written by some full-on hard-core anti-mormon professor who works right here at Harmon Community College."

"And?"

"The book spells out *all* the Mormon secrets. I can *tell* you what they do in their multibillion-dollar temples."

Her eyes went wide. Was this really private knowledge? The only thing she knew about the Temples was that her friends would go there sometimes on Wednesday nights to do baptisms. That, and the most important thing of all, of course; something Tamara elucidated now and then, not to mention how she illustrated the message by hanging postcards of Temples not only all over her bedroom but in the locker they shared as well: Girls and boys go to the Temple to get married.

Jess held a hand in the air. "Maybe you shouldn't tell me, Ryan."

"Of all people, Jess, *you* want to know." He pulled her to a stop and leaned close enough for her to smell the old Juicy Fruit gum in his mouth. "In the Temple, Mormons get married stark-raving naked!"

"No … way."

He laughed. "The whole party, Jess! In the buff, like the day the doctor brought them into the light and slapped their baby bottoms."

"The professor said that? In the book you have?"

He squinted into the blue, which glowed deep beyond the snowy thunderheads above them. "Well, you could always look at it this way: Doesn't matter what side you're with—bride or groom—at least you see what the other is getting."

Shaking her head, Jess started away again. "That's disgusting, Ryan."

"Hey," he said, a doggy that wouldn't split, "*My* name's not Joseph Smith. *I* didn't make up their religion."

"And this professor guy, he's a Mormon?"

"Ex," said Ryan, though he had that look on his face that told her he was probably filling in the blanks where his knowledge ran short. "Listen ... I realize things got rough for a spot with us—"

"You tried to touch me," she said, loud enough for too many other people to hear.

She caught the staring eye of at least two passing football players. But when Ryan, who was the team captain and quarterback, shoved both curious studs away with his dark eyes, they disappeared into the crowds.

"Jess." Ryan leaned against a locker.

In electronic pulses from her hip, Jess's cell phone played out the Miley Cyrus remake of "Some Enchanted Evening."

"Hang on." Brushing some of her dusty-blonde hair— fake dust and fake blonde, but who knew, right?—behind her right ear, she lifted her cell to the side of her face and turned. "Hello?"

"Jess."

It was a boom of thunder, deafening, showering away all the other sounds around her.

Chris.

She swallowed. She didn't speak.

"You're at lunch, right?" His voice trembled, as secretive and quiet as it always sounded, with an added intensity that made her think FBI agents with dark glasses and guns waited for him outside the front doors of his workplace.

"What's wrong," she said.

"Oh great," said Ryan, though he couldn't possibly know who had called. He rubbed his left temple and rested against the lockers until an overweight kid who needed to blow his nose coughed to make Ryan get out of the way. Instead, Ryan growled at the freshman. "What do you want?!!" The kid shook his head and walked off.

And Jess turned around to cut out the school and its complexities from her life. She focused on Chris's breathing. "Tell me."

"I'm sorry for calling you at school," he said a second later. "Jess, I need your help."

Chapter Nine

He could have called Kat. Even Tam—Chris could have called her. But Chris called me!

"Jess?" Tam gave a nudge. "You still in the car with me, or did I lose you somewhere."

Jess blinked, saw the glass an inch from her nose and then smiled at Tam. "Sorry."

"Not a problem, girl." Tam turned onto Broadway. "I'm sorry about last night. Are we okay?"

He called me. Why not Dave. So what if he doesn't have a phone. Chris could have found some way to contact him. They were probably getting together later anyway. Oh, my heart is beating so hard!

"Jess?"

"Yeah? Oh, yeah." Jess flipped the sun visor down and examined her cover-up. If she didn't have enough, she would be as red as a pickled beet all the way to Good Guys and probably worse once she actually stood in front of Chris.

I'm going to HELP him, she reminded herself.
Chris said he would explain everything.

And Tam is staring at me.

Jess grinned, laughed a little. "I'm sorry, Tam. It's just been … "

"No need to explain, girl," said Tam. "It's all my fault. I should have been a better friend."

Chuckling, Jess put a hand on her shoulder and squeezed. "Tam, you're the best friend a girl could ever have. Say no more, sweetie."

They pulled into the parking lot, and Tam shut off the engine. "I'll come in with you."

"You don't have to," said Jess.

"You mean you don't want me to?" She laughed and mischievously slapped Jess on the thigh. "You go girl! Men love confidence in a woman."

Jess grinned, and the smile faltered.

"So what's your plan?" said Tam. "You going to march right in there and smack a big kiss on him?"

Jess caught Tam blinking away her secrets. Pretending that she hadn't noticed, she sighed big. "Wouldn't that be nice?"

"Want me to wait? Or is Chris getting off soon?" Tam checked her own makeup in the rearview mirror, flattening out her lips to inspect the liner before adding a little touchup.

Jess popped the door ajar. "You go on, Tam."

"Okay," she said, starting the engine. "You call me if you need a bailout?"

"I got your number."

Before Jess could shut the door, Tam reached across the seat. "Girlfriend?"

"Yeah, Tam?"

The seriousness on her face made Jess hold her breath.

This was it, said those eyes. *Now for the big secret. Now for the explanation.*

Jess glanced at the door. *Do I have enough time to hear it?*

She looked back at her friend, who wrestled with what words to say. "Tell me."

"Follow your feelings, Jess." Tam swallowed.

Was that *what she wanted to tell me?* Jess thought, doubting it as Tam continued.

"You'll do what is right, if you're true to yourself." Tam offered a corny grin.

"Hamlet?" said Jess.

Bursting into a laugh, Tam said, "Blame Mr. Pierson. He's forcing us to *eat* Shakespeare for breakfast, lunch, and dinner these days. Call me later?"

"You bet." Jess shut the door, and Tam pulled away.

Wait! Jess thought, almost lifting a hand. *Maybe you shouldn't leave me here ... alone.*

Standing in a parking lot that smelled of exhaust mixed with yummy fries from the Carls Jr. next door, she clamped her eyes shut and concentrated.

He could have called Kat.

Even Tam--Chris could have phoned her.

But he called me.

* * *

The sound of a magical bell jingled across the ceiling as she entered.

On wide-screen televisions to her left, Sean Connery chuckled and turned away. The face of a laughing woman appeared before the scene changed and the music swelled.

Then a live person in a blue shirt with a nametag appeared. He clapped his hands before his chest. "And what can I do for you, young lady? Laptop? Blu-ray? HD!" He snapped his fingers in the air—the cracking sound was so loud, Jess jumped—and he said, "I know!"

He waved her in one direction.

She followed, scanning everywhere else. *Please take me to the Chris section*, she said in her head. *I'll take an armload, if he's guaranteed to work. I won't even need a receipt; I have no intention of returning the product.*

"The new iPhone!" the fellow said.

Other Good Guy's employees stood before DVD remotes, stereo equipment, and camcorders, discussing the intricacies of this, the outstanding added features of that, and the always-wonderful-to-hear truth that these were the lowest prices and if patrons found a better price elsewhere, the Good Guys would beat it!

Yeah, I think Chris will be enough, thank you. And can you step on it? I'm eager to get going, if you know what I mean.

As the salesman continued to ramble about the handy little device before her, Jess furrowed her brow and checked the primary sales room again.

Chris was nowhere to be found.

Chapter Ten

In the office upstairs, Chris said to the boss, "Can I have a break sir?"

Bernard Truman, a hairy man with facial growth in all the wrong places, leaned toward the security screens and squinted. "You never ask for a break, Chris. You just don't want to be disturbed for a bit, is that it?"

"Well—"

"I know something's afoot, Christopher Noble. I *smell* these things," said Mr. Truman. And of course he did. Not only was everything around him a mystery-to-be-solved at all times, but he surrounded himself with Agatha Christie novels, *Ellery Queen* and *Alfred Hitchcock* magazines, and even puzzle books on lateral thinking. And he was regularly right.

As owner of the store, he demanded that all employees keep their hair short and their beards cut. Girls could not wear nose rings, tongue rings, nor wimples and crisping pins—he was a man of the Bible. He also said that since customers would see the managers he hired instead of himself, he didn't need to abide by the same standards.

But he liked the growing Mormon boy. That was apparent. He often looked at Chris as if he couldn't quite figure him out. Rarely had their discussions run toward religion. Most of the time, as with most people in fact, Chris kept to himself. He could see how this intrigued his boss even more.

Mr. Truman knew Chris would serve a mission for his church someday. So why be all hush-hush now?

Truth was, Chris never knew exactly what to say. He wanted to share the gospel, sure! Yet here was an intelligent man who took everything and everybody apart for analysis.

Was it a lack of faith that made Chris's tongue stick to the floor of his mouth? Was he scared of getting fired? Or was he just plain weak in the knees because he'd never spoken to anyone about truly sacred things before? He hadn't even really talked to Dave, and that was his best friend.

What had the scripture said last night? "It becometh every man who hath been warned to warn his neighbor."

"Ah! Would you be wanting a temporary cessation from work so you can get to know that little girl right there?" He pointed at the security monitor.

Chris swallowed. "I already know her."

"Jess?" said Mr. Truman.

At the sound of her name, Chris jolted backward. "How did you—"

Mr. Truman tapped the side of his cauliflower nose. "Let it be forever known: I pay attention to my employees," he said with a wink.

Clearing his throat, Chris said, "So may I—"

"Well, I don't know. It looks to me like Ken's about to sell her on an iPhone."

"She won't buy it."

"Got to let him try."

"Okay," Chris said. "I'll buy it for her."

With a thunderous laugh, Mr. Truman slapped the desktop. "Get down there, young man. Don't let that fish get away."

"Thank you, sir."

* * *

Jess had turned to go, but the bewilderment in her eyes made her look like she wasn't quite sure where she was headed.

Chris had told her he would give her a ride home if she came. He really needed to catch her now.

"Jess?" he said, only a couple steps behind her. He kept his voice down, maybe a little too much.

He couldn't be sure that she had heard him at all.

With her hands on the door, she gazed through the smoky glass.

When she turned her head, her hair flipped up and flew over one shoulder. It landed soft and light brown and golden with the sun. "Oh," she said, as cool as ever. "I thought I'd missed you."

He looked at the ground, then around at the security cameras that he knew were watching. That was fine. He felt safer inside than out. "Thanks for coming."

"What's wrong, Chris?"

"Wrong?" He was still a bit scared, but felt a new warmth swelling inside.

Could he tell her?

Did he have a choice?

She grinned at him, shaking her head. "You said … you needed my help."

"You're here," he said, stealing a look at her again.

Slowly, she nodded. "I'm here." For a moment, she scrutinized him in silence. She shook her hands at her sides. "What is it, Chris?"

He couldn't raise his eyes. Something about her was too powerful for him to see, but he couldn't pin it down. Was it simply her spirit, shining too brightly beneath all that outward beauty?

Each time he looked at her, his heart burned. More than anything, he wanted to hold her. And he wanted to stand a little taller whenever their paths crossed. These weren't lustful feelings. The only reason he felt guilty at all was because she was a non-member, while he … well ….

"Chris!" Jumping out of her skin and holding perfectly still at the same time, Jess shook her head and started to laugh. The chuckle turned into a face of pain—not for herself, but a searching ache, a longing to know his struggle, to heal. It was the face of a true friend. Even a best friend.

"Did you write me a letter?"

"What?" she said, but the glow in her eye made him unsure. Was she testing him? Or was this something far worse, the horror that had ruined his morning and lowered his sales.

He pulled the notebook paper from his back pocket. Embarrassed by the folding and refolding the sheet had obviously undergone since he'd first found it stuck under his windshield wipers, he gave a nervous grin and hoped to find some sign in her face.

Yet, like a princess, Jess hid her true emotions.

"Do you recognize the handwriting?" she asked him.

What did that *mean? Was this some kind of game?*

Now, Chris wished *he* had been the one reading mysteries all these years.

"I … I thought I did. The more I look at it, I'm not sure. I mean," he said, "it is definitely familiar. It kind of looks like yours."

She scanned the letter and read a few words out loud: "I'll be wearing something interesting when you see me next?" She laughed. "Is *that* why I'm here?"

"No," he said, though that was partly a lie.

The note was clearly seduction at its best.

He gulped.

If Jess *hadn't* written it, he had to stop this conversation before it made *everything* worse.

Jess pulled the letter from his hands. Her face flushed

as she kept reading. "I've had my eye on you forever, it seems. You are quite interesting! And I know far more about you than you might think. I've been inside your mind, you might say, and had a good look around. And I *like* what I have seen. I want to get closer." With wide eyes, Jess looked up from the letter. "Chris?"

"This isn't … isn't you?"

She didn't answer right away. Emotions and deep thoughts flickered one after another through her countenance. "I guess that depends."

Locking his jaw and drawing a deep breath, he drew close to her. "Jess. *If* this wasn't you … then I need your help to fend off who I … think it might be."

She blinked up at him, tension melting out her cheeks. Her gaze dropped to his mouth, then slipped away as she leaned her head to the right.

"Well, I mean, it *could* have been me," she said with a tone of sly mystery.

Gently, Chris tried to reclaim the letter from her grip and read the last lines. "I'll see you after work someday. I have a little something I've planned, just to get you interested. See you sooner or later … sooner I think."

And Jess read the signature, which wasn't a name at all. "Secret Admirer, hum?"

His face flushed ten degrees hotter. "Are you … Jess … my secret admirer?"

The bell rang as new customers pulled the door ajar.

Not sure how he did it, Chris held her with his eyes.

Yes! her face shouted. Yet her mouth remained soft, lips parted a little and unmoving.

Then Jess burst out with laughter.

"What?" he said. He looked at the letter, which they *both* held in clasped fingers now.

Hadn't he taken it from her?

They were practically holding hands.

She leaned to the left and giggled.

His eyes rolled to one side, then another as he searched his memory for what might have come off so funny.

The customer, who had pulled open the glass door, cleared his throat.

Chris and Jess were in his way. Mr. Truman, trying to read lips from a distance, wouldn't like to see that, no matter how fascinating he might find this new curiosity.

Grabbing her shoulder, Chris stepped her to the side of the entrance. They stood beside giant television screens alive with color, music, and horses at the moment. Some of them boomed the sound of NFL madness.

She patted his chest twice. "Sorry," she said, her laughter uncontrollable now. "It's just what you said! It sounded like lines at a marriage. 'Do you, Chris, take Jess to be your secret admirer?'"

It hadn't been THAT funny.

Chris didn't let her go. He leaned closer, pulling her to him as if that might still her chortle, and spoke with words barely louder than a whisper. "I didn't really think it was you, Jess. You have more class than this."

That shut her mouth.

She looked at him with doe eyes, and they filled with glistening wetness. *Tears of joy? Or something else? Shock of horror?*

"But that means it was probably Rita Hirsch ... who wrote it. You know her?"

She nodded, and her voice came out husky and romantic, though it surely had not been intended that way. "Your ex?"

He averted his gaze in embarrassment and grinned. "Good Mormon boys are not supposed to have steady girlfriends. But in this day and age, a girl and boy in the church don't have to be steady. They'll see each other every morning in seminary, every Sunday at church. They'll meet at each fireside meeting on Sunday nights—that's a little get together—"

Shaking her head, her face serious again, she touched his chest to stop the explanation. "Tam's told me about them before."

"—and at every dance, of course. Then there's mutual on Wednesdays, and—"

Jess splayed her fingers against him now, not to push him away, but to hit his stop button for good. It must have been disconcerting to her: Chris realized he had never rattled on and on like this in front of Jess before, but he was really scared. He couldn't help it. And—her hand was so warm through his shirt now, his muscles relaxed at once.

"Just ... what is the point, Chris," she said.

He leveled his eyes with hers and stared for a moment, building his determination. "I wasn't the best Mormon with her, Jess."

"With Rita?" She cocked her head to one side. "Isn't this something you should be telling your bishop?"

He grinned and looked into the wall over her shoulder. "It's nothing like that."

"Good!" Jess said, smiling with him. "Last thing I need is a dirty Mormon on my hands!" Her face grew red again.

When he drew quiet again, she matched his move and waited.

Swallowing, he nodded with his eyes shut, then looked at her. "If it was Rita. She'll come after me. That's bad. She's the kind of girl who will do damage if she can."

As observant as always, Jess glanced up at the domed security cameras. "Get you in trouble with your boss?"

"Maybe," said Chris, relaxing a little more as she began to understand—and also with the realization that she had most likely not written the letter. That familiar penmanship must have been Rita's after all. So why had he thought that it came from Jess's? Some kind of fear attached to … to hope? Or did he just have Jess too much on the mind?

"Would she try to get you fired?"

Chris bit the inside of his cheek. "She's pretended more than once to still be … with me, just to put me on the spot. At church, you know. And in front of my parents. That sort of thing."

Jess hummed in thought. "And if she comes in?"

"I need … I was hoping you could … "

"Be your girl?" she said.

Chris opened his mouth. *Yes! Yes, that's it, Jess!* You *have been in my head. You've taken a look around and … and …*

He cleared his throat again.

What am I thinking?!? he said to himself.

"Be   your   steady   girlfriend," she   said, "just   in   front   of   her.   To   drive   her   off!"

He smiled as the chimes began again overhead.

"Well, well!" said Rita in the doorway. In a black miniskirt and white blouse, Rita stood, painted like a mannequin dummy that would probably make Jess gag and laugh inside, both at the same time, but also cause a dark arousal in every young man who saw her.

Desperate, Chris refused to look at her but could find nowhere else to turn his eyes … except into Jess's face.

Jess gaped at Rita. Chris watched her brain ticking away quickly behind her outer beauty. Then Jess studied Chris's through the sides of her eyes.

His mouth quivered as he tried to speak. "I—"

Standing on her toes, Jess turned, lifted her mouth to his, and kissed him.

Chapter Eleven

Her lips still there, still on his, still, but not still, quick and hard, and yet soft at the same time, gentle, soothing, telling Chris everything would be okay, saying, *I'm here for you. I'll help you. I ... I ...*

Jess pulled away.

Oh no, she thought when she saw his eyes. *I've ruined everything.*

"Well!" said Rita Hirsch, crossing her arms in the doorway. The back of her head hit the glass with a hollow thump.

Jess heard it, but never took her eyes out of the deep blue Chris stared down at her. *Yes, OUT OF his eyes*, she thought. *Because whether he is shocked into anger, or whether he feels I have helped at all to push his old girlfriend away, I am still in there.*

And I don't ever want to get out.

She almost kissed him again, instinctively, only barely stopping herself before she moved.

What happened?!? she said in her mind.

I SAVED him.

Did I?

I held him, kept him safe from that bad bird of prey in the doorway. I held him without hands, without arms, but with my spirit. With my will. With my lips.

Oh, no.

He'll never be able to look at me again.

"Are you two finished?" said Rita. "If you, like, want me to wait outside under clouds that just might dump rain on us when we talk, that's fine. I just need to know, okay?"

Chris tried to turn his head. It jiggled a little atop his neck, fought to move. But he didn't take his wide eyes away from Jess's gaze.

With no other boy had Jess felt so helpless and powerful at the same time.

In one motion, he took a breath and slid his chin forward and down as if to kiss her again. At the same time, he blinked and spoke and turned his head to Rita. "Did you need to talk to me?"

"You got the note, didn't you?"

"Your note?" he said.

Rita laughed and slapped one of her naked thighs. "Ha! Don't flatter yourself. Professor Cooper phoned me last night."

Are you all right? Jess wanted to say.

Chris swayed, lightheaded it seemed. *Was it the kiss? Was it something Rita said? Was it a combination of good and bad, and if so which had been the good part?*

Thankful that nothing had slipped from her mouth,

she sighed at Rita with eyes both relaxed by the wonder of the moment and annoyed by the interruption.

"He wants to see you." Through her open smile, she chewed her pink gum, then gave her eyebrows a bounce and jerked her head toward the parking lot.

"Professor … Cooper?" Chris said. "Wants to see me? Here?"

"He asked me to arrange a meeting." Rita's nod was more of a musical bounce. "Let's go." She shot Jess with a corpse-gray glance. "You can come too, pretty girl. I am more than certain he'll be quite overjoyed to see you as well."

"Stay here," said Chris. His hand touched her and gave a little push as he stepped toward the door.

Jess glued herself to his skin. She had come to help. And she had no idea how, because she had no clue what was going on.

There had been too many secrets up to this point, and it was time for answers.

"I'm going with you."

Rita rocked her hips out the door.

Before Chris touched the glass, Jess said, "Who's this Professor Cooper."

Chris gave her a protective look then pushed the door ajar. To Rita, he said, "So how do you know Cooper?"

She laughed back at him and said over her gum, "I'm dating his son."

"Chris?" Jess dug her fingers into his arm.

Chris gave his eyes to her once more. Instantly, they were bound together, reaching for heart and soul through their eyes. Without moving, he was wrapping her with both arms while she had her arms locked around his back.

I love you! she screamed inside.

In her heart she heard him respond.

He swallowed and looked at the sidewalk at their feet, then across the parking lot in the direction Rita rolled.

Leaning against a PT Cruiser, a man in gray slacks and a white button-down shirt set free at the neck waited with arms folded, his left foot crossed over his right, and a wide grin stretching across a sunburned face.

"Who *is* he?" Jess said one last time.

A great weight shadowed Chris's face as he stared across the asphalt. "The man's a virus. He makes it his business … to destroy young Mormons."

Chapter Twelve

"Christopher Noble?" The professor pushed off the car and strode with great swooping steps to meet him half-way. "You know, I *just* heard about your big show last night! Rita here doesn't seem to know anything about it."

Rita Hirsch put a hand up to the older guy's ear and whispered in quick bursts.

"I don't think I should be speaking with you," said Chris. He held his ground.

Jess pressed close behind him. He felt her warmth pressed against the hand he let hang loose at his side. Warmth against the growing cold.

This *was* an assault. Chris knew that, yet fought away the urge to shape defensive fists. He was supposed to be an example.

Especially to nonmembers like Jess.

"You shouldn't be speaking to me. Not without your lawyer, you mean?" The college instructor let his flat smile stretch across the width of his face. "Have no fear, young man. I'm not here to arrest you."

"Then what do you want."

"Chris," said Jess, like his conscience. A tremble issued from the back of her throat. "Let's go back inside."

Her fingers clawed once more at his shirt, scratching against his skin in a way that made his muscles jittery and strengthened a longing to turn and press his lips against hers again. Though he doubted she would let him, for real.

He stood motionless, frowning at the professor.

"Let me introduce myself formally." The older man lifted a hand of friendship, the warm gesture so commonplace at church. "Diamond Cooper, professor of Religion and Social Sciences, Harmon Community College."

Chris only looked at the proffered hand. His head came back up at a slight tilt, and intentionally he stared at the old man. He examined the graying hairs thinning atop Cooper's already half-bald head. With open contempt, he studied the guy's free-hanging shirt. And he took a good long look at the prof.'s beaten shoes. "I know who you are."

Righting himself with pride and fabricated dignity, Cooper said, "You've sat in one of my lectures? At one of the local sanctuaries, perhaps? Or have you read one of my books?"

Chris didn't say anything.

"Ah!" said the professor. He passed sly eyes to Rita. "Silence speaks libraries of information. The words of the dumb oft describe the man."

"Then you've heard enough from me." Chris turned and started back through the smell of rain and burgers towards the entrance to his place of employment. "Let's go,

Jess."

"And who might you be, young lady?" said the older gent.

"Don't talk to him," said Chris, his words hardly a mumble.

He had to get her out of here. He should have never walked outside.

But Jess had *kissed* him.

Play girlfriend, he had said, yes. Like, hold hands or something. Laugh and slap his arm and give him a poke in the gut. Maybe even let him put his arm around her—just for show, of course. But she had opened her mouth and pushed off the ground and locked lips!

And then she had stayed there, perfecting the act in front of Rita.

That didn't bother him as much as the granite-hard truths: It sure had felt real, and he liked it.

It had lasted only a couple of seconds. But in those seconds, entire worlds were created, fell, received baptism, hope, and then got celestialized in that moment—worlds without end!

And he couldn't bear it once it actually *had* ended.

His head spun. He hadn't thought clearly: He had come outside with Jess fast behind him.

He grimaced, kicking himself mentally.

Then Jess turned to face the balding professor.

Chris started to say something, anything, as her mouth opened to speak. But at the same moment that she whipped boldly around, the wind blew. The smell of exhaust from the street and deep fried potatoes from Carl's Jr., and even the scent of impending rain, vanished to make room for a perfume of flower and spice and the electrical sight of Jess's glistening skin.

Knocked back, and astonished to see his hand clasping hers, Chris again panicked at the immovability of his tongue.

"My name is Jessica Singer, Professor Cooper. And my father *is* a lawyer." She spoke with feigned innocence on her face. "So if you think we need one, I could make a quick phone call." Quick from the front pocket of her jeans, her cell phone came up in her hand. She brandished the glowing screen like a weapon.

And that was when Chris realized Jess was trying to protect him. She couldn't have a clue what was going on, and yet there she was! Her own best friend had kept Chris's secret from her. He knew why. And he knew that Jess was sharp enough to know something was happening before their relationship could get off the ground and take flight. *After last night*, he thought, *she must have questions.*

Yet there she stood, cell phone in hand, ready to call a man that Chris had never met, and all to protect a Mormon she had kissed because he asked her to—

My gosh, he thought. *I ASKED her, didn't I?! Not with words directly. But I'd wanted it so badly, I must have said it all with my eyes. Professor Cooper is right: Silence speaks libraries of information. I've said too much.*

Folding her arms, Rita leaned towards the professor and spoke loud enough for Jess to hear. "According to my good buddy Ryan Stokes, Jess's father is old enough to be her grandfather—he retired years ago to a wheelchair. Isn't that right, sweets? Is he *still* practicing law?"

How could Rita know all that?

Chris looked from his ex-girlfriend to his ... to Jess.

Jess stood with her mouth open and nothing coming out. The wind blew again, swaying him with the scent of her spellbinding fragrance, and tossing her hair in beautiful ocean swells that glistened with golden light as the sun beamed down from heaven.

Floating away from Chris and then towards him again as if moved by the breeze herself, Jess shut her mouth and blinked to break eye contact with Rita and Cooper.

Had Jess lied? Chris wondered. *Had she exaggerated to threaten the evil duo off?*

The only thing a lie does is promise misery later, Chris's mother had once told him.

He squared his shoulders and told their balding assailant, "I think you should go now."

The professor raised both hands to protect himself as if on the verge of getting attacked. At the same time, he laughed. "Whoa! I intend no hard feelings, young Master Noble. Just a simple inquiry."

"About what?"

"I need a college student for a certain study I am conducting."

Chris smiled with one side of his face. "Forget it. Find your guinea pigs elsewhere."

Before he could turn again, the professor lifted a finger. "Oh, I don't really *need* your permission, Chris."

"Don't you?"

"Oh, no! Observations are made ... and printed ... all the time, young man. Reporters do it. Scholars of all sorts. Specialists in sociology, and even religion." He took a step forward and gave his mile-long grin again. "*The people*, as they say, *have a right to know*."

Jess's hand loosened and almost dropped entirely from Chris's grasp.

Then, shifting position, she matched her palm with his. Her fingers slid through his and gripped his knuckles like a vice.

These were words, he realized. But they were girl words, female telepathy, *Women Are from Venus* stuff. He didn't understand what she meant to communicate.

"A right to know *what?*" Jess asked the older man. Her voice was different now. Strong, yes. But also uncertain.

Without taking his eyes off of Chris, Professor Cooper raised his hand like a shield. "Why a good young Mormon man of your ever-interesting age is *making a display*, not only right here in the parking lot of a small shopping center, but also on the edge of Sunrise Boulevard in front of a half-a-dozen local employees from around Blaine's Burger—wonderful boys who sure like to talk—to name a couple things."

"A *display*? I think you've got a perception problem," said Chris.

"Do I?" Cooper glanced from Chris to Jess. "A Mormon boy on the edge of an exciting and perhaps exotic adventure, here, holding hands with his new Catholic girlfriend."

Rita scowled. She sneered when Chris's eyes jerked to hers.

"What about your *standards*, young Master?" said the professor. "What about the example you are setting for the little ones in Primary? And did you really think that show last night would *impress* people? Do you believe your neighbors to be so shallow?"

"Show?" said Chris. *The oil*, he thought. *The blessing. He must be talking about the blessing. Chris thought he had blocked the view.*

What did it matter anyway? He was doing the Lord's work, right? It was only his second time—the first being a blessing he helped his father give his mother who'd suffered from a mild cold on the night he received the priesthood. *So what* if people saw? He didn't care. He didn't have to. Did he?

"Show—my, yes!" said the professor. Then he grinned super-white teeth at Jess. "Did you think, Chris, that it might convert your little girlfriend to the Worship of Joseph Smith?"

"No," said Chris. But that hadn't been the right word. What would Jess think?

"Jessica Singer?" said the intruder in their millisecond romance. He lifted his eyebrows. "Did it work? You gonna convert?"

Chris lowered his head and hardened his brow without removing his eyes from the professor. "Why did you want to talk to me? Spill it."

"Very simple," said Cooper, obviously relieved that they were finally getting down to business. "It is my intention to write the *true* coming-of-age story of an LDS boy trying to work his way to manhood in the LDS world. You game?"

"Sorry?" said Jess, blinking as if unsure of what he had said.

The professor leaned at her. "I am going to expose Christopher Noble as an example of the great Mormon hoax." To Chris, he added, "Then the white shirts and ties won't seem so white and pressed anymore. Will they, Chris."

"Why single out Chris?"

Rita squeaked with the escape of a little laughter.

Professor Cooper didn't turn to look at her. He just grinned again. "Don't you already know? Chris is perfect!"

Jess squeezed Chris's hand one last time.

Chapter Thirteen

Jess followed him as far as the glass door.

Letting her hand free, he turned from his place of employment and whispered, "You don't have to stay." Chris looked over her head. "I'm sorry I got you involved. I had no idea."

"No, Chris," she said, as if this was a daily occurrence in her life; old hat. "Not a big deal."

Without removing his eyes from Rita and Cooper, he said, "Well it might become one. I've heard enough about this guy."

"Like what?"

"Like every member of the Church of Jesus Christ of Latter-day Saints ought to keep a safe distance from him." He pulled the door open.

"Why?" Jess swallowed. "What are you really afraid of?"

He stopped, turned a bit, but didn't meet her eyes. "It's not fear, Jess. He's trouble."

"Well, as the old crack pointed out," Jess said, "I am not a member of your faith."

Chris lifted his eyes and lingered on her for a moment. She saw pain rising out of his confidence, and she wondered if she had said the wrong thing.

"So," Jess said to correct the situation, "he can't touch me."

But the drill of his eyes, the ache of longing she thought she saw, reached right inside of her mind and throttled her heart.

They were still connected. Whatever magic had lit between them, the flame had not vanished. She had felt his lips with her own. She still smelled his after-shave. She had touched her soft chin against the invisible whiskers spiking out of his cheek. She had rubbed fingers and palm against his. And when her hand had grown sweaty during the verbal assault, she had felt his also moisten. Jess was inside of him.

"If Professor Cooper is going to publicize my life," Chris said, "he'll name you in his study as well … because you are a part of it."

Her voice only a whisper, and without any permission from her brain, slipped out of the back of her throat loud enough for him to hear: "A part of your life?"

He almost nodded. Instead, his trembling hand slipped off of the door.

Tinted glass slowly closed between them.

He did not look away from her.

Powerless, she couldn't take her eyes off of him. She started to reach out, to press her hand against the cold pane separating them.

It was the hand still holding her cell phone that came up. She looked at the device, wondering who had put it there.

Chris saw it. He rolled his lips into his mouth and tasted them.

Was she still there? A memory on his mouth?

A desire welled up inside of her: not to open the door, but to smash her arms through it.

No more separation.

No more secrets.

Only Chris, only Jess, only together.

"Thanks for coming," Chris said through the glass.

Jess didn't hear him so much as read his lips. She wanted to burst with laughter and weep at the same time. She blinked once and shook her head twice. "Not a problem, my friend."

Then, inside, she screamed.

Friend?!? I've said the *worst* F-word!

She spun around and flipped her cell open and stared at the numbers as she began to walk—where … nowhere!— as if she'd never used this phone in the past.

Call … who?

Tam? Tam was ready for both the 911 and the 411 that would necessarily follow.

What would Jess tell her? She knew. Through hours of tears and frowns and terrible trauma, she would say, *Chris loves me*.

It was true. Jess had felt it in the way his skin vibrated and caught fire against hers. He'd stood forth to protect her, and she had done the same for him—or at least, she had tried before making a fool of herself. How could she know that Rita Hirsch had been spying and doing background checks?

Why in the world would Chris's feelings be a problem, then?

It was something else, the great secret, that kept them apart.

And now this anti-Mormon grownup was out for blood and humiliation. Could he do that? Was it really necessary that Chris push Jess to arm's length at all times? Hadn't he rushed an inch and a half forward after she had kissed him, ready to kiss her again, to forget the Ritas of the world and the playacting and the—

Or had it only been a sham … the sort of drama mastery Tam would have been proud of?

Had Chris fooled her completely?

She squeezed her cell phone with angry fingers. *Why won't anyone tell me anything?!?*

But Jess was sure she already knew the truth. It was just that some of the pieces didn't fit.

It was probably as simple as what she herself faced, but had never openly recognized: her father didn't press Jess with endless commandments. In fact, he only had one wish for her that mattered to him. "Make me a promise," he had told her years ago. "If you love your old man, you promise me this one thing."

"Yeah," she had said. "Anything, Daddy."

From his wheelchair, he had leaned forward, shaking with the Parkinson's ailment that had taken him ten years earlier and had slowly worked its way to a constant jittering in his face. "You go to mass, Jessica. Every Saturday night, you listen to Father Dundan, shake everyone's hands, say 'Peace be unto you' with all the rest, and take communion like a good girl. If you do that, I'll not worry about anything else you do in this life. Will you go, young lady. Will you do that for me?"

She had promised, and only one time had she broken that promise: the evening of the Valentine's Day Dance at the Mormon chapel on Colville Road.

Because Chris had asked her.

Kind of.

And Jess had not expected her father to find out.

But when her ex-boyfriend hadn't seen her that night—and because of the romantic holiday, Ryan had been looking—he had gone right over to her house on Kenyon Street and had engaged in an innocent little chat with her papa.

Telling her daddy later the truth had been torture. Not only had she violated her integrity in his eyes, Jess had gone to a *different* church.

And that was the problem, wasn't it?

Tam … Dave … Kat, certainly … and maybe even her cousin, Ben—they all had stated at one time or another that Mormons can't marry non-Mormons. Similarly, if Jess even hoped to marry Chris Noble in one of those super-white LDS temples, her father would likely roll away from her and give up the ghost halfway down the hall to his bedroom.

At the same time … Tam had arranged the date last night. But she had basically refused to reveal the Mormon secrets when they started to appear.

Jess had gotten too close, she guessed.

She had seen things not meant to be seen.

Oh, she thought, *this is so frustrating*.

Jess watched the PT Cruiser spin out of the parking lot.

From the passenger window, Rita blew her a kiss and waved her long nails against the glass.

Jess stared at her feet, which had stopped in the center of the crowded asphalt field.

What am I doing?

What was I thinking!

How could I have hoped … ?

"Jess?"

She turned.

His foot wedging the door open, Chris stood in the entrance of the Good Guys.

No! Jess shrieked inside. *It was only an* act.

But if so, Chris sure looked like he was still playing his amorous part.

His eyes implored, called her to come back, *hoped*. His face leaned away, just slightly, with uncertainty.

"I'm all right." She smiled. She held up the phone. "Tam must have her cell turned off. She was headed home anyway, so I'll give her a couple of minutes and call her house. Interesting weather, isn't it?! I mean, look at those clouds! Blinding white, some dark as ash and charcoal, and there! Blue sky, and the sun escaping from time to time. You think it will rain?"

I'm rambling. I sound like an idiot.

Chris didn't look at the sky. "I'm getting off in forty minutes."

"What?"

"It's kind of a long wait, I realize," he said without breaking eye contact. "But…." He looked into the store, then drew a breath, expanding his chest under his work shirt. He let go of the door and strode right up to her.

She trembled. She couldn't take her eyes off of him. She didn't remember any of her thoughts anymore. He was staring at her.

Without any semblance of a smile, but a weighty seriousness on his face, Chris looked right into her eyes and spoke with a soft voice. "If you can wait, I'll … I'll drive you home. We can get something to eat on the way. And …"

Her hand jumped up. The tips of her fingers lighted upon his lips to silence him.

Oh my gosh, she thought. *Did I just do that?*

As she lowered her hand, he caught her fingers and cupped them with the gentle curl of his own.

Her mouth was already open. "I'll wait for you, Chris."

He shut his eyelids. When he lifted them again, his eyes glistened with extra wetness.

Entwining his fingers into hers and without taking his eyes off of her, he led Jess back into the electronic entertainment store.

Oh Chris, Jess sighed. *Is this really happening?*

His blue eyes spoke back: *I don't know what's happening anymore. But you're here.*

I'm here, she replied. *I am* here.

Chapter Fourteen

What am I doing! I can't let this happen.

Chris dropped his receipt on the counter. The scent of the hot *churros* covered in cinnamon and sugar permeated the air around him. The sound of grilling patties of beef seemed to hush him, to tell him that he should relax, that this wouldn't hurt a bit.

But wouldn't it?

"Forty-one?" said the Blaine's Burger employee, a short man with a goatee and a gold ring hooked through the side of his nose.

Chris tapped the slip of paper and then took the tray of hamburgers and fries. He smiled as he wandered back to the small table in the corner of the dining room where his date waited.

Jess turned her head a little left, a little right, gazing into a small pocket mirror and dabbing at the edge of her lipstick at the corner of her mouth.

Chris's smile faded. His heart galloped under his blue shirt. When Jess looked up at him (magically making the compact disappear), he pulled the smile back onto his face.

"Did they get it right?"

"Better than last night," said Chris. "They'd put onions on my burger instead of cheese. I must have had breath that could kill flies yesterday."

"I hadn't noticed," Jess said, and she seemed to be struggling with the same difficulty as Chris: the more he looked into her eyes, the more he found his smile displaced by a powerful reverence and awe. He ended up staring. And she was staring right back.

"Probably didn't smell it because I kept my mouth turned away from you as much as possible."

"Oh!" she said, as if that had explained some mystery to her.

We're not getting together, Chris told himself. *We can't. It just couldn't happen.*

"Here you go." Chris passed her one hamburger with extra bacon, one Sprite extra fizz, and one bag of french fries extra small.

Three of the fries spilled onto the table.

He reached to pick them up, but Jess got there first and his fingers caught her fingers instead of the tumbled food.

And he didn't let go.

Mostly, because he forgot to.

His eyes went from fries to her hand to his fingers and then to her face.

With lips parted and breath held silent, Jess was looking right back at him.

He felt her fingers wrap around his.

"Jess," he said. He shut his eyes and opened them only enough to gaze at the table.

She started to speak. "I—"

"Jess, there's something I have to tell you, before this goes any further."

Swallowing, she said in her husky voice, "I already know."

He looked up.

Someone told? Well of course someone did. How could it have remained a secret. Who was it then, Kat? Katrina Martinez would have been on the front lines, he knew that. *Maybe Dave let it slip. He was an awesome friend, but a little dimwitted at times. Or what about Tam?* Tamara Cline and Jessica Singer had been kindred spirits since elementary school. Chris knew that too. He had been watching Jess for that long.

"You know," he said.

"Well, yeah. And don't worry about it. I won't get in your way."

Chris nodded, then leaned over the table. "Jess, you have *never* been in my way." He held his breath, then spoke again. "I've … liked you for years."

Slow on the take, Jess seemed to be replaying the words in her mind. "Years? Like, since when."

"When?" said Chris.

She looked at their hands, still clasped. She put a hand on his, locking it there with a gentle touch. "Can I ask you something important, Chris?"

"Sure. Jess, anything." Chris blinked, knew the words had come from his mouth, then thought, *Who just said that?!?*

Her eyes came up again and kissed his. "I … feel something."

"A con—" he began to say, before his breath totally gave out. He started again. "A connection."

Nodding, she said, "Like I've known you forever, even before I was born."

All right, that's it, Chris shouted inside. *Jess has hung out with a lot of LDS friends over the years. But there is no way she KNOWS about the Preexistence. And that was a MORMON thing to say.*

His head growing light, Chris imagined his spirit slipping out of his body and leaving a corpse on the ground.

Jess had *not* knocked the wind out of him. She had vamped his life right into her hands.

"This can't be happening," he said, gazing wide-eyed at the table again.

"Right," she said. "But is it?"

"Is it happening?"

"Romances don't start this way," she said.

"Romance," he repeated, unable to think. He was in her eyes again, and she inside of him.

How did his free hand get on top of hers?

His heart thundered, thrashing around like a wild animal inside his ribcage. It beat against every muscle in his chest and shoulders and arms. It flushed his face so that he thought he saw the steam rising up, but that would ludicrous—*this CAN'T be happening.*

"A relationship doesn't begin so quickly," she said without blinking her amazing brown eyes.

"Yeah."

"Unless this one started weeks or months ago."

Chris took a breath. "Or years."

With her eyes innocent and honest, Jess said, "So when did you first notice me?"

This can not *happen.*

Not now.

"We shouldn't …"

"I know," she said. Her hands slipped away as she examined them. "I know." She checked her watch.

"Do you need to be getting home?" he said.

"Well, I don't have anything important to do. I mean, other than homework. Help my Daddy around the—"

"You were at a birthday party," Chris said, still in a daze, reaching with his eyes and hoping she would look up at him again. Yes, there was a connection. And to rip that bond in two would be like cutting his gut out and chucking it across Sunrise Boulevard, into the ditch where the missionary had fallen last night.

"Where?" she said, joining her soul to his again across the table.

"I don't remember whose it was. I saw you there, in a dress. With pink shoes."

"Pink?"

"A yellow dress. You were running. In the backyard. A big sheep dog had taken your cake right off the table and gobbled it down. And you were chasing the mutt around, a table covered with red and white and blue streamers, and confetti."

As he spoke, Jess's hands rose to cover her open mouth, but didn't quite make it.

"Your … pigtails. They were all brown then, perfectly combed," said Chris. "And they bounced behind you as the grownups tried to slow you down, then tried to catch you."

"Chris!" she whispered. "I was only *nine* when I wore that dress, those shoes."

He nodded. "The most beautiful girl I had ever seen, even when the dog—who thought it was all a game—climbed up one side of the picnic table and down the other to get away from you."

"And I followed it!" She grinned with nostalgia and shame.

She laughed music that yanked Chris back in time. He saw all the other precious moments when that open laughter played in his ear. He had always remained at a distance.

In his mind, Chris was back at the party, and yet here at Blaine's Burger talking to Jessica Singer over food that was growing cold.

"You were at that party?" she said, and the words sounded like she was covering something up or evading something he had said.

What did *I say?*

"You saw me? You remembered me?" she said.

He nodded, a zombie caught in her spell.

I have to break free, he thought.

But slowly, he said, "That's when I knew I would some-day m—"

Stop!

Stop it!!!

In a whisper, she prodded him. "You would what, Chris?"

He looked at her watch.

There was something …

"Oh my gosh," he said, glancing around for a clock to confirm the time. Of course, there wasn't one. Restaurants, even as down-to-earth and homey as this one, never seemed to hang clocks where customers might see them. "I completely forgot."

Jess pulled her head back, blinked, and nodded. "You have somewhere else you need to be." She looked at her food, the burger still wrapped tightly in yellow paper.

Chris put the heel of his right hand to his temple. "I told Dave I'd meet him."

"Sure," she said.

After grabbing his fries with one hand, the cheeseburger with the other, he stared at his drink, and it hit him how this might sound like an "I've got to run home and wash the rugs" excuse to get out of this spontaneous and overpowering date.

Jess stood when he did. She gathered her things without looking at him.

Ah, man. "Jess?"

"Oh, don't worry about it," she said. "Like Ben says, 'Food on the run is half the fun,' eh?" She sighed at how lame she sounded.

"I can … I can take you home real quick—"

"Well," she said, rushing after him to the exit.

"Or … ." He pushed the door open for her, but his hesitation gave her pause.

Thunder banged in the multicolored afternoon sky.

"Do you want to come with me?"

Chapter Fifteen

They entered the hospital holding hands.

Jess wasn't quite sure how their hands became clasped together, but then things were *happening* all by themselves today without any permission from her.

In this case, he had taken her hand when they left his mother's Prius and headed across the parking lot. He had been looking up at the blue patches they could see in the sky, while scant and amazingly heavy raindrops began hammering down around them.

When the double doors slid open at their approach, he didn't bother letting go, and she didn't want him to.

Chris must have known where he was headed. They marched straight past the information desk and right to the elevators.

So as not to be heard by any of the transient patients and green-garbed hospital workers, she pressed close to him to speak. Being this close meant that Jess had to lean her head back to look into his eyes. And that reminded her of the kiss. "Is there anything I should know?"

He swallowed. His eyes darted to the faces around

them. Something made him nervous. He spoke low and quiet. "Just stay close to me, Jess."

She smiled, almost laughed, and sighed it away as the warmth of his arm pressed against hers. "Don't worry about that, Chris. I will *never* leave you."

He looked down into her eyes.

"Not for a second," she said.

His eyes bounced to her mouth.

She looked at his.

They were too close. It was going to happen again. And this time, no question about it, it would not be an act.

The elevator bell rang.

The metal door swung wide.

"Excuse me," said an orderly pushing an old woman in a wheelchair with an I.V. pole and drip bag attached.

Jess started to move backward, to step away from Chris, and let them through.

Chris's hand pressed to the small of her back. He pulled her towards him, and thus made way for the older lady and the man in white. They were almost dancing again.

"Thanks," said the guy.

Now Jess felt her whole body pushed up against Chris. Once more he looked down into her soul with those sky-blue eyes. "Sorry," he said. Then he reached and caught the elevator door before it could close.

They went inside, and Jess held his hand as he stabbed a knuckle into the number three.

As the car began to float heavenward, Jess looked up at him again. He was already gazing back at her. And they stood that way until the door opened.

Chapter Sixteen

A moment later, they entered room 324.

"It's about time you showed up," Dave said. Like a couple of dry burrs, his eyes caught on Jess and stayed—he looked like a dealer caught with drugs and new money in his hands.

Dave's sister, Kat, stood silently in another corner of the room, her arms crossed. Kat's eyes widened in surprise when she spotted Jess.

Jess waved a brief hello.

Kat nodded once, though her look of sincere concern regarding Jess's appearance did not fade.

In the hospital bed rested the missionary who had been hit by the car. Instead of a white shirt, he wore a hospital gown covered with little pastel flowers. A giant bandage covered his head, and he had the ugliest black eye that Jess had ever seen.

Dave sat in a chair on one side of the bed next to an older guy standing in a dark suit. The grownup didn't fail to take notice as Chris and Jess entered. He looked like a special agent from the FBI.

On the other side of the bed stood the missionary's companion—the dope who had gone into the dirty drink first, and had thought it funny—and the older guy, a balding man with an awful lot of gray in his hair.

This last fellow turned and grinned at the other visitors. Jess saw a black nametag on his jacket, white letters printed on it: PRESIDENT EDWARD P. HUNTINGTON.

"All right then. Elder Rutter? Elder Smith? Are you ready?" said the President.

Dave started to stand, urgent eyes darting from his best friend to Jess and back again. "Chris?"

Chris raised his hand to make his pal take a seat. "She's okay, Dave."

The standing missionary, who the President had called Elder Rutter, saw Chris, and his face lit up. "Oh, Elder! I'm glad you made it."

"Elder?" said the President with a smile.

"This is the brother I was talking about," Rutter said to President Huntington.

"Well then," said the eldest gentlemen, lifting a hand of welcome.

Chris stood forward and shook his hand.

"We were about to give Elder Smith a blessing. Would you join us?"

Chris swallowed, his eyes skirting the floor in Jess's direction. When they touched her face, the President took three steps towards her.

Dave nearly fell out of his chair. But he was only getting up. To what, though? Protect her? Shove her out of the room?

Her back bumped the door. "Should I—"

"Welcome," the man said, offering her hand. "I'm President Huntington, San Diego North Mission."

She breathed. She smiled, eyes wide. And she took his firm hand. "Jessica Singer."

"Won't you have a seat, Sister Singer?" He guided her to one of the hospital chairs, and she took a seat.

"Thank you."

Chris was staring, his eyes saying, *Everything's okay. Just stay close to me.*

At least, she hoped that was what Chris said in his mind.

Stuffing his hands into his pockets, Dave made room for Chris. As the others circled the bed, Dave got mashed into the corner. He gave Jess one uncertain glance, then didn't bother her again.

The door blew open.

"I'm here!" It was a whirlwind of colors, perfume, jangling keys, and breath mints.

"Tamara?!" said Jess, leaning on the armrest.

Tam's eyes turned into giant circles. "Jess?!"

"You got the door, Tam?" said Chris as Elder Rutter pulled out his keys once again.

"Oh!" said Tam. "Yeah!" She grinned, giggled, and squelched it by clearing her throat. Then she whispered, "Sorry!"

Jess concentrated on the keys.

They were the same keys Elder Rutter had passed to Chris last night.

Now, Rutter took the small brass vial in his fingertips. He unscrewed the part that connected it to the ring itself. Then he set the keys on top of a short hospital cabinet beside the bed.

As Jess leaned forward, the chair squeaked.

More than a few eyes turned.

Grimacing, she froze. "Sorry."

Tam's eyes darted to Dave. She walked to Jess's chair and hunkered down beside it.

"What is *happening*, Tam?!" said Jess.

"Don't talk," Tam said.

"But … ." Jess took the advice, though she knew Tam well enough that for her to squat here like this meant she had lots to say to her best friend.

"Okay," said Tam, her voice so quiet and her mouth so close to Jess's ear that it was hardly a whisper at all. "You read the Bible a bit, right?"

"Tam?!!"

"Shh, shhh! Okay, sorry," Tam said and licked her lips once. "I want you to try to remember back to the stories you read or heard. About Jesus. Jesus and the lame man, Jesus and the blind, the lepers, the sick, the withered, or bleeding."

"What?" said Jess, her eyes not leaving Elder Rutter

as he moved the small bronze vial closer to Elder Smith's head.

"Remember, Jess!" Tam said. "How Jesus, and later how the apostles just like him, laid hands on the sick … and *healed* them."

Jess opened her mouth.

Tam covered it.

In Elder Rutter's careful fingertips, the vial turned. Beneath the opening, the missionary held one finger.

A drop of colored liquid, too thick to be water, swelled into sight at the edge of the brass vial. Then it fell to Elder Rutter's fingertip. Another drop followed. And then another.

And as the third drop came down, Elder Rutter lowered his finger and the vial of oil—*That's what it was; That's what Chris had said last night; that's what … what the Bible described the apostles using after Jesus' death, wasn't it?*—until it reached the crown of Elder Smith's head and disappeared from Jess's sight.

Tam lowered her hand, then her head, as she folded her arms.

Jess quickly folded her arms as well. She bent her head as if in prayer, but couldn't take her eyes off of the proceedings.

While all the others stood in a solemn circle around the hospitalized missionary, Elder Rutter set the vial next to his keys.

He swallowed.

With fingers slightly spread apart, he lowered both hands onto his companion's head and shut his eyes.

When his mouth opened, his face seemed to concentrate hard, as if listening to a voice very far away. And he spoke: "Elder Richard Smith. By the authority of the Melchizedek Priesthood which I hold, I place this oil upon your head which has been set apart for the healing of the sick in the household of faith." He ended in the name of Jesus Christ, then said, "Amen."

Everyone in the room said, "Amen." Everyone except Jess.

"I didn't know I was supposed to participate," she super-silent whispered at Tam.

Tam leaned close. "Just as in ancient times, Jess, we say 'Amen' if we agree and support what has just been said by someone giving a prayer."

"Okay." Jess could understand that much. At least she hadn't been kicked out of the room. Not that it had not almost happened, however. Dave was stuck in the corner, and the Mission President had sat her down himself and called her *Sister* Singer.

They think I'm a Mormon, she said in her mind.

Chris wants me to stay close, doesn't plan on shutting me out—thank goodness.

Dave would have done so already, if he could have.

Tam seems to be caught in the middle, but at least she's leaning my way now!

"What's happening?" whispered Jess.

All of the men, except Dave, closed in on Elder Smith. Their arms went up. Each placed their hands on the hurt missionary's head, all at the same time. *The weight*, Jess thought, *must be crushing!*

"Oh, that was only the beginning!" said Tam, faintly. "Listen ...."

Though she couldn't quite see anyone directly but Chris (who shut his eyes in an expression of both peace and concentration), President Huntington spoke this time.

"Elder Richard Smith. In the name of Jesus Christ, and by the authority of the Holy Melchizedek Priesthood which we hold, *we* place our hands upon your head and seal this anointing of oil, and offer you a blessing. Elder Smith, the Lord, your Father in Heaven, has called you to serve in this mighty work, to carry forth the wonder of the restored Gospel of Jesus Christ. Your time here in the field has been long, but not long enough. The Lord still has need of you, for many who might hear and follow the beckoning of our Savior will yet only do so when you arrive at their door. Remember, Elder Smith, 'Many are called, but few are chosen.' You have been chosen to perform the work at this time and in this land. In order to help you press forward in these great labors of the Spirit, I pronounce this blessing upon you. I bless you to heal, Elder Smith. I bless you, in the name of Jesus Christ, that you might rise up ... and walk."

Jess blinked. On television, she had heard people talk this way. In movies, even at mass sometimes, she had heard holy men speak in the name of God.

But this man spoke with *authority*. His words came out relaxed and confident, as if he had perfect faith that what he said would come to pass.

"Amen," said the Mission President.

The word jolted her. She had tried to wait for it, ready to say the word with the rest of them. But her mind had wandered.

As quickly as she could, she blurted out the word. "Amen!"

Everyone else had already said it.

Tam drew a quick breath.

Dave studied Jess from around the crowd.

Chris looked at her with sincere interest in his eyes.

She glanced at each of them, and then said, "I agree." She blinked as tears came to her eyes.

Agree? she thought. *Yes, I do! I support what was said. I have a hope. Even, if I'm not one of you. I* really *hope Elder Smith heals. He has a work to do.* Jess felt her skin tingle with a wave of goosebumps.

Tam put a hand on Jess's arm, and she started crying. She smiled at her friend. "Yes he does, Jess. He has a work to do."

Did I say that out loud?!? Jess thought with her lips pinched shut.

Yes, she had. It had only been a whisper, but replaying the moment in her mind, Jess *heard* the words slip from her throat: "I support what was said. I have a hope. Even if I'm not one of you. I *really* hope Elder Smith heals. *He has a work to do.*"

Trembling, all on fire inside, Jess wiped away a tear. "What work?"

The Mission President looked down at her. Wise parental love radiated from his face. "A marvelous work, Jessica Singer, and a wonder!"

In the minutes that followed, Elder Smith shook hands with everyone in the circle who had participated in the blessing.

Tam didn't say anything.

Dave still couldn't move.

Chris seemed to glow with light like everyone else who had used 'the authority of the Melchizedek Priesthood', as they had called it. Was it the hospital room's lamps, or just a sensation?

Jess felt weightless. She wasn't even sure that she sat in the chair anymore. And the words spoken around her blurred into a fuzzy warmth.

I'm fainting, she thought, but then didn't lose total consciousness. *I must be fainting!*

"Are you okay?"

She blinked and found Chris's face close to feel his spearmint breath on her skin.

With concern in his eyes, he held her head as it rested against the wall. With two fingers, he wiped away tears on her face.

She wanted to reach up and brush his hands away—

she would *never* have fallen into such an awkward position of stupor like this before! Not in front of Chris.

But she forgot about moving, and only remembered the circle of men laying hands on the head of the bed-ridden Elder Smith.

She heard pieces of the blessing in her mind: *Elder Smith, the Lord, your Father in Heaven, has called you to serve in this mighty work, to carry forth the wonder of the restored Gospel of Jesus Christ.*

She heard Tam's whisper from only a few minutes ago. It seemed like years, or like it hadn't happened at all, and yet Jess remembered every word: *Remember, Jess! How Jesus … laid hands on the sick … and healed them … the lame man, Jesus and the blind, the lepers, the sick, the withered, or bleeding … and healed them …*

"Jess?" said Chris.

"I'm okay," she said, fresh tears sliding free from her lashes. She smiled and hooked one hand over his wrist.

"Let me say goodbye, and I'll take you home."

She nodded.

But as he walked away … *she saw in her mind a dusty street with old buildings rising to the left and right. Crowds had gathered on the dirt road, and a man was coming. Everyone was looking at him, shouting in words she didn't understand. And reaching to touch him. And one, on the side, on his knees, looked up with eyes that were permanently shut. "Master!" he said, though his lips moved to make different sounds as he spoke in an ancient language.*

Dressed all in white, Jesus Christ stepped from the crowds and looked down on him.

"Please heal me," the blind man implored.

In the Savior's eyes, compassion took the place of sympathy. He lowered his finger onto the blind man's face.

Wait! Jess said in her mind.

That look in the eyes of Jesus Christ. That look of sincere love and also power. It had been that same look she had seen in the eyes of the Mission President.

She shook her head.

Imagination! she said.

"What?" said Tam.

"Nevermind." Jess felt liable to slip away again into the feeling of warmth and peace all around her, but she didn't want to leave Chris.

If she got the chance, she would ask for explanations. But that would have to come later.

After President Huntington shook her hand and left the room, she stood. Chris, Dave, Kat, and Tam had gathered around the bed. They laughed about the accident with Elder Smith and told him everything would be all right now.

When Chris said he needed to be heading out, Elder Smith shook his hand one last time. "Chris."

"Yeah," Chris said.

"I just want to thank you again," said Elder Smith.

"Who knows," Elder Rutter said, swatting Chris on the shoulder. "Without your help last night, Elder Smith here might not have made it to the hospital alive."

Chris gave a little smile, but humbled his face and looked at the floor. His toes inched toward Jess.

Dave, on the other hand, seemed to grow dark in the corner again. With his hands stuffed deep into his pockets, his nostrils flared as he gazed up at the wall.

"You too, guy," said Elder Smith, shooting Dave a look.

"Well, we were in the vicinity." Dave shrugged, then shook hands when the Elders reached for him.

"Chris!"

Chris was halfway to Jess now. He turned his eyes back.

"How long've you held the priesthood?" said Smith.

"Since Sunday night."

Elder Smith nodded. "You put your papers in then."

Papers? Jess asked herself. *Did I hear that right? What does* papers *mean?*

Chris's volume dropped a notch. "Yes."

"Ah. That's great," said Elder Smith.

"A marvelous work and a wonder!" said Elder Rutter, thumping Chris in the shoulder.

"The field is white, all ready to harvest," said Elder Smith. "I'm almost envious. To be in your position!"

"Sweet," Elder Rutter added, nodding.

The excitement in the air was electrifying, doubly so by the polar sensations of the Elders cheering while Dave, Kat, and Tam stood cold and quiet and unmoving. Chris was somewhere caught in between.

"Papers?" Jess said out loud.

Chris took her hand to go, but stood at her side to tell everyone goodnight.

"What papers?" Jess said, asking anyone, everyone.

Both missionaries, Dave, and Tam stood staring in silence, now, right at her. Kat sighed at the window.

Chapter Seventeen

Chris didn't escape the room without a number of insane looks, especially from Kat, whose eyes shouted, *What in the world are you DOING?*

If there had ever been a secret sect of Mormon Police, Katrina Martinez was a special agent. Dave's sister really was a good girl, but if she could force everyone into heaven, she'd be glad to try.

And this couldn't look so good.

But appearances are deceiving. And right now, Chris didn't want to think about how the others might be judging him. He would hear it all soon enough.

"Chris?" said Jess during the quiet ride home.

The rain had begun to fall again. A light mist on the windshield kept the wipers busy.

"You must have questions," Chris said.

Oppressively low storm clouds had turned the sky to night almost two hour early. All the street lamps had lit up, and every car had its headlights blasting.

"It's okay," she said. "You don't have to tell me anything that's … secret."

Chris glanced at her. "There's nothing secret about my religion, Jess. Just a few things that are so … sacred we don't normally talk about them."

She nodded. "I trust you."

Do you? he thought. An overpowering wave of warmth slammed him, and he knew it was true.

"I can *ask* things, can't I?" said Jess. "You don't have to answer, of course. I mean, I don't want to make you feel uncomfortable or anything."

He looked at her again and fought off an urge to take her hand and hold it. "Anything, Jess. Please."

"All right," she said. She spoke her next words with confidence, though she sat all weak and almost dumbfounded in the seat next to him. "Catholics talk about something."

"What is it?"

"The Holy Spirit. Old people sometimes call it the Holy Ghost." She gave a silly grin of embarrassment, as if that term had been a Catholic secret in itself, secret because the word 'ghost' gave the impression of some half-embodied apparition floating unwanted though hallways upstairs, moaning from time to time about something lost in life, or worse: some horror flick's version of a malicious poltergeist out to ruin the lives of the living.

"What about it?" said Chris, wishing he had paid a little more attention in seminary. He thought he knew his stuff pretty well. He had almost finished reading *The Book of Mormon* all the way through on his own for the first time. And he had asked a lot of questions himself. But she might ask something he hadn't learned yet. After all, he had yet to go to the Missionary Training Center. *Who knew* what the Elders learned there, except those who had already gone?

"I … thought I … felt something in the hospital." She crumpled into her seat as if she'd just revealed the nakedness of her soul. Uttering a quirky laugh on her breath, she said, "Nothing spooky. I'm not saying—"

"No," said Chris. "I felt it too."

She examined his face for a while.

Chris wasn't sure he should look at her or stare straight ahead. A discussion about something like this was serious business.

This was missionary stuff.

Maybe Kat had done this a dozen times.

It was even possible that Tam had testified to someone at school, possibly even Jess in the past.

Certainly Jess's cousin Ben Wainwright wouldn't have talked like this to Jess. Ben had always slept straight through seminary in his pajamas, and he almost never went to youth activities during the week.

And no way in the world had Dave talked to a nonmember like this before. He was still smack-dab in the middle of his conversion.

Chris didn't want to mess this up. So he told the truth. "It's hard not to feel the Spirit when someone is exercising the Priesthood. Outside of the Temple, I've rarely felt anything so powerful. Not yet, anyway."

"*You* felt it?" said Jess. "I wasn't even sure what I felt, but I thought … I mean, I had heard Kat say one time … that it was like a warm feeling inside, overpowering."

"Overpowering." Chris nodded. "You've said that twice. It's been an overpowering day."

"*Days*, if you ask me." Her fingers touched his arm, then withdrew.

She shook her head. "I definitely felt something in there. Something I have never felt before. But you have?"

He nodded. "I've felt the Spirit so many times this last year, I'm starting to wonder if older Mormons just get used to this sort of buzz."

She squinted at him.

Glancing at her, he cleared his throat. "Doesn't make sense, does it."

She waited.

"I was baptized when I was eight years old—"

"That *late*?" said Jess.

"Yeah. You could say that I didn't join the church until I knew the difference between right and wrong."

He saw the logic and light flash in her eyes.

"Anyway, I grew up in the church. But that doesn't mean I always had a firm understanding of what we believed, or that I even believed everything that I heard in Sunday School."

"What do you mean?"

"Well, have you ever had *questions*?"

She shook her head. "I don't know."

"When I was younger, I usually didn't think much about church. My parents brought me on Sunday. I became a Boy Scout through church. You know, that's where I really got to know Dave."

"Right," said Jess.

"But that doesn't mean I *believed* everything. I didn't even *think* much about it all. And when I did, it all seemed so *big*. I mean ... have you ever been in your bed some night, stared at the ceiling, and tried to picture in detail what it was like where we lived before we came here?"

Jess shifted. "Here?"

"To Earth."

"Where we lived ... before?"

Chris cleared his throat again. "Yeah. I mean, the Preexistence. Or have you ever asked yourself *why* you are here on Earth?"

"Me?" said Jess, her voice almost a whisper.

"Or where you're going after you die? What it will really be like up there? What we will do, what we might *learn*, who we'll be able to see ... and be with, forever?"

She stared at the road.

"Well," Chris said. "I didn't think much about those kind of questions when I was younger. The older I got, though, the more I started to wonder. And I can understand why some people *don't* believe in God."

"Atheists?" said Jess. "You?!"

He smiled at her. "I said, I think I came to understand

them." He faced forward again as the headlights of a passing car burned across the rainwater on the windshield. "It is *easier* to believe there is no God, *because then you don't need to answer those three questions.* And you don't have to follow *any* commandments. It's like, if you were delusional enough to think you didn't have parents, then maybe you could ignore their rules."

"That's pretty harsh," said Jess.

"But it's true. Because Heavenly Father *is* up there. And He really sent His son to Earth."

"His son?" said Jess.

"To die for us," Chris said. "I know it's true now. I … found out. Ever since then, I have felt the Holy Ghost with me all the time."

"Like … a guardian angel?"

Chris slowed the car before a red light and looked at Jess in the dark-pink glow it cast upon her face. He half-smiled. "I'm sorry, Jess. I shouldn't be talking about these things with you. You're not a Mormon."

"But I *asked*, Chris." She took his hand. "I *want* to know about you."

He looked at their entwined hands and firmed his fingers around hers and felt the warmth radiating through her soft skin.

"I want to *know* you, Chris," said Jess, softening her voice. "I want to know everything."

Her face changed under the green light.

With her eyes so sincere and lips so yielding, Chris

wanted to lean over and kiss her. He ached inside to move his arms around her. He longed to hold her, to squeeze her to him and feel her arms wrap tightly around his back.

And he knew she would, if he moved a centimeter.

Oh, I want to, he said in his mind.

But I can't.

I shouldn't.

And with that, Chris didn't move until a car horn shook the air and made both of them jump.

He looked at the intersection and the green light.

When had that changed?

He put his foot on the gas. The wheels spun a little too much in the rainwater. The car listed to the right before jerking forward. The light turned yellow as they passed beneath it.

They drove for a minute in silence.

"You could talk to the missionaries," Chris said. The idea came as a whisper in his heart. He couldn't manage a conversation like this. He could testify, sure. But he wasn't even sure he could teach her correctly. He could tell her what he knew. He could tell her that he loved her with all his heart—

I can't do that!!! Chris told himself. *WHAT am I THINKING?!? Get a grip, boy.*

"Missionaries, ahh," said Jess to her feet. "My father would never go for that."

Of course, Chris said in his mind. *Why did I say that?* "Your father. Right. I've heard."

"From whom?"

Chris shrugged. "Tam, I think. She's protective of you, you know."

"A little *too* protective sometimes." Jess folded her arms.

"I'm sorry, Jess." Chris turned onto Kenyon Street where she lived.

"Don't, Chris. There's nothing for you to be sorry about."

"Okay," he said, glancing at their hands. He was driving one-handed—*very bad*, said his brain. *Very good*, said his heart. *But if I don't die in a car crash before reaching her house, my parents will kill me if they find out about our little hand holding.*

Chris had taken the long way, on purpose, which meant they now had a whole lot of stop signs to go through before reaching her block.

Chris wished to spend more time with her, sure. He also wanted to see if Jess might correct his route and get herself home faster, or if she wanted to linger with him.

"Can I ask you a question?"

"Sure," said Chris, pulling to a stop and waiting for the ants to march by the front of his car (Yet another red light, though there weren't any other cars in appearance).

They were getting close now, so he took his time.

Jess lifted her chin a bit. When she looked at him, her eyes came up innocent and honest, totally open and willing to connect. "What's 'Hold to the Rod' mean?"

"Hold to the Rod?" He grinned.

Was she kidding?

"It's a Primary song. Where did you hear that?"

"A *what* song?"

"It's something kids sing at church." He shrugged. "Adults too, now that I think of it. I don't know. Maybe it's not a Primary song at all. Am I thinking of something else?"

She crossed her legs and set her face straight-ahead. "Look, you don't have to tell me about it if it makes you feel uncomfortable, Chris. I understand."

He would have laughed, but he cared too much about her feelings. And it had been such a ... such a *day*, both wonderful and unnerving. "No. Jess, it's not a problem. Hold to the Rod ... it's an idea based on a vision that a prophet had a long time ago."

"I've never heard of it." The words came out a little too fast, and he wasn't sure what to make of her altered tone.

"You wouldn't. Not unless you've read *The Book of Mormon*."

With her free hand, Jess ran her fingers through her long golden hair. "So what's in it?"

"What?"

"In the rod." Now she sounded like a detective digging for information, like an agent who thought she already had the answer but was testing to see if Chris would tell her the truth.

The air chilled in the cab. "I ... like I said, it's an

idea, a commandment, kind of." He didn't know what to say. Where in the world had she come up with *this* question? Had she read one of Professor Cooper's anti-Mormon tracts? Was this some kind of weird trap planted in the sort of miscommunication and lack-of-context and confusion promoted by the enemies of the Church?

Jess hummed once in thought.

Chris licked at the back of his bottom teeth. "The rod represents the Word of God, the scriptures. Keep to the scriptures—reading, pondering the messages, praying about them—and it will hold you to your course. Does that makes sense?"

She shook her head and kept her eyes forward. "It's okay, Chris. You don't have to tell me."

The skin on Chris's face grew cooler. "I thought I just did." In his mind, Chris saw Kat's hard face and her I-told-you-so expression.

"No, you don't have to tell me, Chris. It's fine." And Jess really did make it sound like everything was okay, that he didn't *have to* tell her.

But Chris felt the foundation under his feet shifting and giving way. "Tell you what?"

"What's *in* the rod. It's oil right?"

He blinked and shook his head. "There's nothing in the rod, Jess."

"Nevermind."

"Jess—"

"No, Chris. Let's ... let's forget I asked the question."

He cocked his head to one side. They were on her block now. "Jess, I—"

She turned her head suddenly and leveled her eyes on his temple. "Will you just tell me one thing?"

"I know what you're going to ask." He straightened himself in his seat. His hand was sweating so badly against hers, he hoped her fingers wouldn't stink later. And now the issue of his papers had arrived. "I thought you said you already knew about it, that Tam or somebody told you. Kat maybe."

"Was it just an act, Chris?"

That tripped him. He looked at Jess a little too long. The honk of an old F-250 turned his attention back to the road. He swerved to avoid hitting a parked sedan.

Jess had tears in her eyes. Her face contorted with pain that she failed miserably to hide away. "Was it, Chris? Because I thought … well I know that *I* kissed *you*. But I thought I felt—"

He lifted her hand between them and gave it a gentle squeeze. "Jess. I'm floating so high right now … we'll be lucky to make it home alive."

She stared at him for a long time. "Then maybe you'd better put your hand back on the wheel."

When he pulled in front of her house after fifteen super-long seconds of uneasy silence, Chris stopped the engine and turned his face toward hers.

Immediately, an unexpected gravitational force began to tug at their lips, to pull them towards one another.

Their pain just wasn't a barrier that could stop the swell of desire. There was so much Chris was unsure about, and so much uncertainty in her eyes, and yet *still* there was a connection between them. And he really was floating.

Never kiss in a car, boomed the voice of his bishop from a fireside that Chris had attended last year.

With the heat of her mouth reaching his before her skin could, and with the smell of her perfume all around him, he jerked his head back, spun around, popped the driver's door open, and fell onto the street.

He thought he heard a sound, a tiny squeak before he rose and shut his door. It could have been anything of course, but he thought it came from Jess. It could have been a little laughter. It could have been a miniature eruption of weeping. Either way, Jess stayed inside the Prius, no doubt stunned by this peculiar Mormon action he would not be able to explain if he tried.

I shouldn't be doing this, Chris told himself. *That's the problem. That's why there is so much emotion ripping us both to pieces right now. This* can't *work. We can't be together, and that makes our relationship the forbidden fruit both of us can't live without. We are so different. And yet we are the same in ways that she couldn't possibly realize. We need each other.*

He banged his fist into his forehead to stop the mad rambling of thoughts.

He didn't know what he needed to do anymore. He only knew what was in his heart: The Church was true. God needed him right now to participate in something wonderful and powerful. And Chris was insanely in love with Jessica Singer.

Walking around the back of his mother's car and opening the passenger door for her, he offered his hand in the drizzle of rain that he hardly felt.

Jess tried to avoid his eyes as he pulled her to the sidewalk. Her desire to see him won out, however, and so Chris saw the uncertainty. She looked away and started rambling. "I went too fast," she said.

"What?"

"It's my fault, I realize. Not yours. I mean, *you* called *me*, of course. But there at the Good Guys, it was like, Here's my problem. And then—Bam! Rita's standing right there, the only Mormon girl who wears lingerie in public. And I didn't know what to do to help you. I mean, I didn't really take any time to think about it. And then I'm all kissy-kissy."

Oblivious to the rain coming down in gentle waves over them, they walked up the short concrete path to Jess's front door.

As Jess spoke, and did not stop even to breathe, it seemed, she shivered like a child in the snow without a jacket. She leaned into him, and pressed herself under the warmth of his arms. And she kept her eyes on the concrete, even as water droplets collected across the top of her eyelashes like diamonds.

Once under cover, Chris turned her to face him as she continued trembling and talking. She stared at his wet shirt. "I didn't know what to do," she said. "Or I wasn't thinking. And so it's my fault, not yours. I really should have thought about it. I put you in an awkward situation. But I didn't like the way Rita was looking at you, like some prostitute who expected you to melt at her feet and hang onto her ankles."

"Jess," said Chris.

"And it really was only a second—half a second!—maybe even less. I don't know. But I was *supposed* to do something, right? And so, yeah, I think I did the right thing. Kissing you, I mean. But you don't need to think anything about it because, I mean, between you and me, I'll be honest. There really is, I mean, I really—"

Her eyes floated up his neck to his chin, his mouth, and finally his eyes.

"—I love you."

His own hands shaking, but not because of the cold, he cupped the side of her jaw and leaned close, leading their mouths together in a soft kiss.

It lasted an eternity.

Chris felt tears itching to come forth.

When he finally pulled away from her two or three seconds later, he said, "There. That time … I kissed you."

Jess stared into him. There were no barriers. It was like before, but now he had told her *his* feelings, without words. So there could be no more confusion.

She looked at his mouth again and rose onto her toes and kissed him again.

The front door made a harsh snapping sound as it came free and opened wide.

In the light of the front room, Jess's father sat in a wheelchair. Under a line of gray hair and fat wrinkles, Mr. Singer's hard military eyes split Chris and his daughter into two people. His mouth, drawn into a thin white gash, remained silent.

Chris put his hands into his pockets. He loosened his jaw to say something like, *Good evening, Mr. Singer.*

Instead, the force of the old man's gaze pushed him backward and his feet carried him off the six-inch porch and back to the cement walkway.

Chris looked at Jess, dripping and shivering and alone in the porch light of an early stormy evening. He smelled the tiny purple flowers on the bushes along the base of the house. And somehow he caught the scent of her perfume lifted by the wind off his own clothes and skin.

"Goodnight, Jess," Chris said, walking backward, quickening his pace.

Her lips parted. Her eyes, large and longing, followed him.

Chris wanted to ask if he could call her tomorrow or something. But he turned to the car and saw her, quiet, trembling, and motionless through the rain.

Jess stepped over the threshold and hung onto the front door before Chris could free the car keys from his pocket. Then, looking into the house at the wheelchair rolling out of sight, Jess shut the door and turned off the light.

Chapter Eighteen

"Hello, Singer residence."

"Jess? Is everything all right? You sound like you've been crying." Tamara Cline paced between her bed and the dresser as soon as she started talking.

"You sound like you expected to hear me crying," said Jess on the other end.

"Your cell's out of order again."

"No. I turned it off."

Tam sighed to the ceiling, which she had painted dark blue with pink stars twinkling all over. "I should have told you sooner. I just … when you two would look at each other, it was so obvious to me that you'd get together. Like, it was meant to be. But I should have known it wouldn't work out."

"I was the dreaming one, Tam. But no worries, okay?"

"Are you good, girl?" said Tam, falling forward on her bed. She picked at the yarn rising in intervals from the quilt her mother had made years ago.

"I'm good."

"Hmm. You don't sound too convincing."

Now Jess sighed over the phone. A grumble followed. Then a sliding sound ending with a dull thump.

"Are you down?" said Tam.

When one of their telephone conversations got heavy, Jess went to the far side of the bureau, what she'd dubbed her Hiding Place. Once in position, Jess would lean her back and head against the wall. She slid down the wallpaper and landed with a hollow bang. Her father never asked about it, and Tam called the maneuver 'getting down.'

"I'm down."

"Okay then," Tam patted the bed. "What happened."

"Oh. It's my dad."

"He saw a boy drop you off?" said Tam.

"Oh, yeah."

"And he knew it wasn't Ryan?"

Jess breathed across the line. "My dad can go on hoping about Ryan Stokes, Football Star, all he wants."

"He just looks forward to seeing you married in a Catholic church, right?" Tam laughed a little—after all, everything was out in the open now, right? Nothing more to worry about? Jess had heard them talking about Chris's "papers" in the hospital, and so Chris must have told her everything on the way home, and the relationship was over before it really got off the ground … right?

"Tam … I kissed him."

Cocking her head to one side, Tam wondered why Jess told her *that*. "You kissed your father? What—you never done that before?"

"No, Tam. I kissed Chris."

"What?!" Tam fell off the bed. Completely unaware of her own private catastrophe, she jumped to her feet and started pacing again, knocking a bottle of Too Shy hair color off her dresser and not even caring enough about *that* to pick it up. "*You* kissed Chris?! You've never been that bold with a boy in your life. Girl!"

"I know." Jess blew hot air into the phone. "I know." Her voice cracked. "I was *helping* him."

"Well I'll say, woman! I mean, most guys would *like* a little of that kind of help once in a while, but ... Jess?!?"

"No, you don't understand," Jess said. "Rita came with some anti-Mormon professor from Harmon Community College—"

Tam froze and went cold. "Diamond Cooper?!"

"What. You know him?"

"Heard about him," said Tam. She ran to her window and peeked out the blinds.

Only one car was parked across the street, the blue Honda Civic owned by the Rollins family who lived there.

When a white Ford F-250 drove past slowly in the rain, she pulled her head behind the wall so she wouldn't be seen.

"They used to call him Diamond Slick," said Tam. "He went to some theological seminary years back and tried to become a priest or something, but somehow didn't quite cut it. When we were babies, he went around to a number of different congregations—Protestant churches, only—

and bashed on the Mormons. You know, warning them against the 'Mormon Scourge' and that sort of thing."

"You're kidding."

"Hey, it was a job. Folks would pay him to visit whenever the missionary efforts from my church drew too many friends or family members away from their churches."

"Why would they call a guy in like that. People don't just *hate* people, Tam. This is the modern world, you know."

"Oh, I'm the optimist, Jess. Remember? I'm not saying they hate; they're just working really hard to *save* other people from themselves." Tam looked in her mirror and realized she was using her hands to talk, like always. "To a lot of these guys, *this* is business."

"Huh? I thought it was religion."

Tam made a clicking noise with her lips. "Think of it this way, Jess. I am the pastor of, let's say, 300 locals. If each of them come to my house of worship because I give outstanding sermons, and because I have a great band, and I tell them that they are all saved, just by coming and saying, 'Praise Jesus', then every Sunday, I can pass around my basket and they will *fill it up* with cash and checks for the good of the ministry. Do you follow so far?"

"Sure, Tam. What's your point?"

"Okay," Tam said, her free hand in front of her face as if it helped to illustrate the matter. "I *am* the ministry. These good people pay for the lights in the building. They pay for the air-conditioning. They pay for my house across the meadow. You follow?"

"Right there, Tam. Go on."

"They pay for my car. They pay for my movie rentals—"

"Okay, Tam, I get that."

"In other words, to be a minister is my *job*, and if I do good, they pay me *good*. If I do outstanding, I can live like a king." Tam let that soak in.

"So what?"

Tam laughed. "So *what*?! Babe! Picture this now: If missionaries from the Church of Jesus Christ of Latter-day Saints come knocking at the doors of my flock, some of those doors will open."

"Okay," said Jess, waiting for more.

"And out of those doors that open, some of *my good people* will let those missionaries inside."

"And?"

"And," said Tam, "those missionaries will do something absolutely terrible."

She heard Jess lean close to the phone. "The *Mormon* missionaries? What will they do?!"

Tam smiled. "They will *testify*. And the Holy Ghost will have their backs, filling the room with a light that those good investigators will not necessarily see … but *feel*."

"Oh … my … gosh."

"And then those good members of my flock with join the only restored Church of Jesus Christ on the Earth, the only church with a living prophet—"

"A *what?*"

"—and Twelve Apostles, called by God, given authority through the laying on of hands."

Jess cleared her throat. "You said a prophet, right?"

"Oh come on, girl. You know that already. I've mentioned it a billion times over the years: The President of the Church of Jesus Christ of Latter-day Saints is a prophet."

"Oh, yeah. I knew that," said Jess, but she sounded a bit stunned for some reason.

"Are you all right, Jess?"

"So, you were talking about this *Diamond Slick*, professor."

Tam nodded at her reflection and started pacing again. She watched the plush cream carpet squish up between her toes. "Right. So if I was a minister, and Mormons are *stealing my income*, then I would want to bring in the heavy guns, right?"

"What do you mean?"

"I'd want to fortify my flock against the power of the LDS Missionary."

Jess thought about that for a second. "But how could you do that ... if the Holy Spirit has their backs?"

Tam grinned. "You can't. But you can try. And the Devil will be happy to help out."

"The devil," Jess said across the phone lines.

"Diamond Slick didn't become a professor until we started high school," said Tam. "I guess he could only do so much visiting congregations, spreading lies—"

"Like Mormons getting married naked?"

Tam burst out laughing. "That's a good one!"

"He really said that."

Tam chuckled a little longer. "Doesn't surprise me. I've heard worse things, all these fake secrets us Mormons are supposed to have."

"Like what?"

"Oh, let me think," she said sarcastically. "Oh yeah! Like we hold animal sacrifices in the basement of our Temples." Tam shook her head. "You know, Jess? In the old days, people who tried to get others to hate or fear members of my church used to say things—like we literally had *horns* that grew from our heads, and that we filed them down in secret so that we could blend in."

"Well that's silly," said Jess.

"It is *today*, but a long time ago, I guess people took that kind of stuff seriously. Now days," said Tam, starting to laugh again, "They say we get married naked."

"Well do you?" said Jess.

"Of course not! Though, I bet Ben would love the idea."

"How do you know you don't," Jess continued, her voice serious. "You've never seen a marriage in the Temple before. You told me that."

"No, I haven't," said Tam.

"And the things that happen in there are … are too sacred to talk about outside the Temple walls, right?"

"That's true, toots. But trust me. We don't get married

❦ 150 ❦

in our birthday suits."

"But how do you *know*."

Tam sighed. "Because I've *seen* what we get married in. And … it is beautiful."

"You *have*?"

"And it is sacred, Jess, so I can't talk about it anymore, because I probably shouldn't have seen it in the first place. So don't get me in trouble."

"Can you get in trouble? Are there some kind of Mormon Secret Police?"

Tam exploded again, laughing so hard tears came out of her eyes. She fell on the bed and chuckled on her side.

Jess couldn't help but laugh after a moment. "I didn't realize that would be funny."

"Well, it wouldn't have been," Tam said. "But then I pictured Kat in some white-shirt-and-tie getup with a Nazi band around one arm." She laughed until she started to cough.

Jess laughed with her.

Both had seen Kat enough to know she was a real saint at all times, except when Dave crossed certain lines in public. Then, like a scorpion, she called her brother to repentance. It usually sent him into a silent rage. Or not so silent. But when Kat turned on Tam, Tamara always found a way to put Kat in her place. She usually used the line, "Judge not lest ye be judged, for with what judgment ye judge, ye shall be judged, and with what measure ye mete, it shall be meted unto you again." And those words usually sent *Kat* into a silent rage.

When they stopped laughing and started breathing again—stopped making, *Heil Hitler* jokes in mid-chortle—Jess said, "So why is everyone so freaked out about this professor.

"That's right," said Tam, getting a grip. "Okay. Diamond Cooper got a job at the college, probably because he knew enough influential members of the community. Someone probably worked on the board or something. Maybe a lot of someones. I don't know what kind of schooling Diamond really has. When someone makes a living by lying or speaking evil about a group of people, you know they're not the righteous type—if you ask me."

"So what can he do? Invade chapels?" Jess wasn't making light of this. She sounded terrified.

"Oh, don't worry, Jess. He can't touch you. You're not a Mormon."

"I'm not a Protestant, either. But it's not me I'm worried about."

In the mirror, Tam looked at how much her eyes had bloated because of all the laughing. "Other than what he says in churches around the county and in his lectures at the college, Professor Cooper writes regularly in the local papers. Usually the Back Page, where you find Fluke Angels from Mars, and stuff like that. Anti-Mormon sort of news. I don't read it anymore. I used to think it was funny how he would find a Mormon—*any* Mormon!—who had done something wrong anywhere in the United States, and *publish* it as news."

"What kind of things," Jess whispered.

"You know: Mormon Man Caught in Tax Evasion—stuff like that."

"But now you don't read it anymore," said Jess, "because something bothered you."

"Right," said Tam, lowering her voice. "He started writing about people I *knew*, or knew about. He digs up dirt, then exaggerates it or makes you look at it through a dirty lens so it looks twice as bad. People are afraid."

"Why don't people sue!"

Tam shrugged at her reflection. "Don't know. Maybe they have. Maybe they haven't had good lawyers. Honestly though, I know a lot of the people I go to church with would just blow it off. My seminary teacher read some scriptures to us once that basically said that if you are persecuted because you are a true follower of Jesus Christ, then you should be happy."

"Happy that a creep like that is hacking on you?!" said Jess.

"Because, 'so persecuted they the prophets.' You know: turn the other cheek. That sort of thing."

"Tam? Did you just quote scripture to me?" Jess laughed a little release of tension.

Beaming, Tam said, "Yeah! I don't know where that came from, but I feel smarter already! Kat would be so proud of me."

Jess sighed against her wall.

"You're not getting up," said Tam.

"I told you. I kissed Chris."

"That-a-girl! Way to go! *I'm* proud of *you*!" said Tam. "At least you got something before that fish swam away."

"Away?" said Jess. "He kissed me back. And I think my father saw *that*."

Tam's jaw dropped. Then she plopped her bottom right into the carpet where she had been standing. "He *what*??!"

Jess whispered again. Tam could almost hear the tears starting. "He kissed me, Tam. On the lips. He was … holding my face."

"Oh. My. Gosh."

"And I … "

"You *what*, Jess."

"I told him—"

Tam stood. "Told him *what*?!"

"—that … I love him."

"Oh. My—"

Chapter Nineteen

At home, Kat walked the floor and pressed the heels of her hands into her temples. "This can not be happening."

"Give it a rest, will you," said Dave. "It's not your problem."

"It's all of our problem, David. Think about it. If you knew a child was about to die and you did nothing to save it, *you* would be as much to blame for the child's death as whatever or whoever killed the child."

Dave shook his head and chuckled without sound. "You have been reading *way too many* books, Kat."

She grabbed her scriptures.

"Oh, no." David stood from the kitchen table. "Time to do homework, I think."

Without looking up from her triple combination, she flipped the pages and said, "You *never* do homework, David. I'm your *sister*, remember."

"How could I forget? You've said a hundred times: We are going to be a celestial family, even if it kills you."

"Sit down."

He sat.

"And I never said that." She gave the tip of her middle finger a lick and kept turning.

"With actions, Kat. Not words."

Why am I even doing this?! she thought. *Because I can't solve this problem by myself. I've never been that close to Jessica Singer to begin with. I've tried very hard to keep my closest associations among the Saints or with people who might be receptive to the gospel. And Jess has been* Tam's *investigator for years—not that she's done such a good job with the young Catholic lady. Probably hasn't even given the girl a Book of Mormon yet.*

"Can't find it?" said Dave, his voice grinning a bit.

"Shut up."

"Whoa!" Dave put up his hands. "*You* just said the S-U word." He stood and lowered his hands onto hers.

She shut her eyes. She wanted to scream, but she *had* said the S-U word, a term on her mental list of what she called Mormon swearwords. She had personally vowed to never use those words.

And now *Dave* was coming to her rescue?

"It's Friday night," he said. "Let's put on a video."

"No thank you. I'm not in the mood for vampires or violent action movies."

He shrugged. They were all alone with the television acting as a parent. Jason, a neighbor kid age four, was in the other room. Their mother did not allow them to take money for babysitting, because Jason's father helped whenever the plumbing had problems. In other words, Dave and Kat weren't going out, and they only had each other.

But with parents like theirs, "each other" was all they ever really had.

Mom had learned to blow off the stress of the day by running away with friends that she met in yoga and belly-dancing classes. Most of those women were singles with beer bellies; they had all been married before, and divorced, at least once. Kat had tried to keep her mother away from that crowd—"You are better than that club," she had said—but Kat's words did not prove to be very convincing. Mom still disappeared for hours on end. Kat wondered if her mother had started attending bars with her friends. She worried that Mom had taken up drinking. Yet Kat didn't dare ask, because she really didn't want to know for sure.

Dave took a deep breath through flared nostrils. "I was thinking *Groundhog Day*."

Kat smiled, then frowned the emotion away. "You're only trying to make up for what you said at lunch."

"That's not true." He walked to the video cabinet, then turned back to her. "I've just never seen you like this."

Hunkered over her scriptures, Kat pushed brown hair out of her eyes to see him. "*Is* true. Why don't you say it? You're sorry I don't have a date. You're sorry that I *never* have a date when the weekend comes. I just turned seventeen, and I'm ugly."

Dave aimed a hand at her. "You know, I hate it when you talk like that."

"Hate" was another of the taboo words on her list. It made her shut her eyes, but she listened anyway.

"You're not ugly."

"Easy line, coming from a brother. If you propose to me, I'll throw up on your shoes."

"Don't worry about *that* happening," Dave said.

"Anyway, brothers think their sisters are ugly or pretty, and not a bit of it has anything to do with romance. You can't look at me and see what other boys do." She crumpled into her chair. "You're right. I'm nothing more than a sweet spirit."

Dave shook his head and groaned with disgust.

"*You* said it!" she snapped at him.

"I was being mean, okay? I'm sorry!"

"It was true. I'm too tall anyway. Six feet?" she said, looking down at herself. "That's not human."

"But you're full," Dave said.

She leaned her head to one side. "That's another way of saying I'm fat."

"No," he said, lifting his eyebrows. "I *do* know what other guys like, trust me. Anyway, models are tall." He daydreamed at the video cabinet and the wall. "But as *you* said, I'm not Chris. He'd see something more, I'll bet."

"He never *has*!"

Dave's jaw fell slack. He stared in silence. "You're not … you're not *jealous* of Jess, are you?"

"What girl *wouldn't* be? Chris is the Peter Priesthood sort every Molly Mormon wants, and he's got all the rest going for him too."

"*You are NOT* in love with him," said Dave, walking forward with wide eyes. "All this time and you said *nothing*."

"David, I am not saying anything now. He's … the type … of guy a girl like me would be interested in, is all. And he's never even *seen* me. Not even when I'm sitting on the sofa right in front of him, or in the back seat of the truck. Your best friend!"

She turned away from him and went to the fridge.

When Dave didn't say anything, she looked back at him.

He lifted the DVD with Bill Murray on the cover. "I know how important it is for you to be a Molly Mormon."

"Oh, will you guys please stop calling me that."

"I mean, you *want* to be a good … Sister in Zion."

"Yeah?" She folded her arms.

He shrugged. "I've just never seen you go crazy like this."

She laughed bitterly. *Why was this so difficult for everyone to understand? Why couldn't her brother—Chris's best friend!—figure it out?* "You saw them at the hospital."

He nodded. "So what?" Yet, she saw the concern hiding under Dave's heavy brow.

"Think about it." She grinned. "How happy do you think Chris will be after this relationship shatters all his plans?"

Dave's jaw slid back and forth as his mind predicted

the future.

"Oh, he'll come to you, all right," said Kat, taking a step closer. "He'll come weeping. Won't that make you feel comfortable?"

"That's what you think." He tucked the video under his left arm and stuffed his hands into the pockets of his jeans.

"But what is worst of all," she said, "is the day all Chris's tears dry up. That's when he will look back and see everything clearly. He'll know that *you*, his best friend, could have prevented all that misery ... but did *nothing* to stop it from happening."

Without blinking, Dave stood in the living room for a while thinking.

Kat let a smile play on her face, but only to annoy him. She had to make him *think*. He had to play things through mentally. He had to *see* what she saw. Then he might *do something*. Because Dave looked up to Chris. A part of him *needed* Chris to be an example. And Kat knew it.

Dave tossed the disk onto the couch. Without even a glance, he lumbered into the hall and headed for his bedroom.

Oh well, Kat thought. *Maybe he'll need to spend the night sleepless before he takes action.*

The seed was planted.

"What *you* need, Kat," said Dave's voice from out of sight, "is a little bit of *faith*."

His bedroom door slammed.

Kat stormed into the living room and aimed her mouth like a gun. "Faith without works is dead, David! If *you're* not going to do something … then I will!"

Chapter Twenty

"Jessica? Hi!" said the voice on the phone. It was so sweet, so much like an old girlfriend calling after spending years abroad. But Jess had no idea who it was. "I saw you at school today. That was a really nice outfit you were wearing! I was wondering where you got the pants!"

Rita Hirsch flashed in Jess's mind. She saw the tight top and the miniskirt, and tried to give this voice to her. The polished voice didn't fit the image. "Oh well I ... ." Jess tried to sound innocent, almost comical. Certainly kind. "Who is this?"

"Kat."

The word hit like a straight ruler across the knuckles. *WHACK!*

Kat's stern face at the hospital snapped forward in Jess's vision and matched with the voice. "Kat," she whispered.

And she waited for a moment in the heavy silence, listening to the nothingness on the other end of the line.

Why didn't Kat say she'd seen me at the hospital? thought Jess. *Why did she say she saw me at school instead. We don't have any classes together.* Besides, Kat had always avoided her, grinning and giving best-friend waves from afar, as if Jess were some kind of leper or something.

Sure, for the most part Kat was nice to everyone. But her eyes had grown darker and darker as the months of Jess's senior year rolled on.

This has nothing to do with pants.

So it must have everything to do with Chris.

And Kat still wasn't saying anything.

Of course not. Kat had to prove clean at all costs. She was little Miss Perfect. Her laugh, her smile, her modest dress standards, her grades—Kat really *was* a good person. But she'd never made house calls to strangers like this. And as close as Jess was to this little Mormon crowd, Kat still had never really *talked* to her.

"Does this have to do with Professor Cooper?" said Jess.

Kat's voice grew jittery, though she still spoke with a smile in her tone. "*Cooper*?!?" She dropped an octave. "Why would I be calling about him?"

Oops, Jess though. *I dropped the bag and spilled the beans on that one, maybe. Better watch what I say.* "No reason."

"Because you're not Mormon?" said Kat.

Bringing up Professor Diamond Cooper was a big mistake.

"Well you're not really calling me about what I wore today, are you," said Jess.

After a beat of three seconds, Kat said, "Are you saying

I'm lying?" Her voice really seemed to struggle between the nice girl she wanted to be and the war she felt she had to fight. The tension had been obvious in her eyes at the hospital. And her tongue couldn't hide it now.

"How did you get my number, Kat. It's unlisted. My father has this thing about the government and his privacy."

Kat took a breath. "It took some doing. Didn't seem like anyone would give it to me at first. But your cousin, Ben, was *very* nice to me."

Only because he's a slave to his desires, Jess thought with a hand on her forehead. "Did you tell him you just *had* to talk to me on a Friday night about my pants?"

"Oh, no. He's *worried* about you, Jessica. He said you totally freaked on him at lunch today."

Jess sat on her bed. "And is *that* why you called? Because you're worried about me too?"

"I'm worried about Chris."

"Because I'm the enemy?" said Jess. She wasn't really going out on a limb. Jess expected an attack like this from somewhere, from her father in particular, but not so soon.

Even her dad had only asked a few questions before leaving her alone: *What's his name? So this is serious? How long have you been kissing him? Why didn't he introduce himself? Is he Catholic? He's WHAT?!!*

Kat's voice intensified; she must have put her mouth right up to the phone. "Listen, Jess. It is ... important ... that you stay away from him. He's going through something quite serious. And he doesn't need some crack in the sidewalk to make him stumble at this point."

"Oh!" said Jess, pressing a grin into her own voice while folding her arms. "So I'm a crack in the sidewalk, is that it? Thanks for calling. It never would have been clear to me had you not put it in such beautiful words."

"Please, Jess," Kat said, then surprised her with a cordial laugh—best girlfriends again—and a sigh. "You are a great person."

Now Jess pushed *her* mouth to the phone. "You don't even know me."

"But I really want to help Chris before—"

"Before?" said Jess.

"Before things go too far, is all," said Kat, still keeping her tone as positive as she could. She probably would have done a better job if she had gotten involved in drama with Tam. But then, Jess was sure Kat would find it sinful to kiss guys on stage, even when acting.

"Too far," said Jess. "Help Chris." She scratched her head. "Did he call you today at lunch?"

"What? No."

"After school, maybe?" said Jess.

"No."

"Just now?"

"No, Jess."

"You mean … Chris never *asked* you to help him?"

"No but—"

Jess stood. "Well he *asked* me, Kat. He called *me*."

"To hold hands with him at the hospital? To mess up his concentration during the blessing? To snuggle against him in front of us all?"

"I think it was *your* concentration I messed up during the blessing, Kat. Chris did fine."

Darker than ever before, Kat said, "How would *you* know?"

"I think this conversation is over." Jess moved to press the off button on the phone. She stopped when she heard Kat's tone change.

"Jess," she said, almost a laugh, almost a tear-filled voice, totally sincere this time. "I'm sorry. I haven't been handling this correctly. Please?"

"What," said Jess.

She heard Kat swallow. "I just want Chris ... to be happy, is all. And this ... is a very delicate situation."

"I think he is happy, Kat."

"You don't know what he is going through, Jess. You've never seen this happen before. You've never seen how it can mess up a family, tear it to pieces from the get go, and leave only what *looks* like a family behind."

Jess waited, listening as Kat fought to control her exposed emotions.

"You don't know how it can hurt children later."

"What are you—"

"My mom married someone who wasn't a member of the Church of Jesus Christ of Latter-day Saints," said Kat.

"But your dad's ... a Mormon, isn't he?"

Someone sniffed. Jess imagined Kat dabbing her eyes with a Kleenex. "He wasn't when they got married. In time, he joined the church. He promised to get sealed to my mom in the Temple. But they never made it that far. And now they're hardly married at all. And my mom … is not …."

"Kat," Jess said with a soft voice. "I … had no idea."

Sniffing again, Kat restarted her happy voice and added as much strength to her shaky tone as she could manage. "Jess. Do you love Chris? I mean, for reals?"

Jess nodded before she answered. "Yes."

"Then you can't get in his way. Or he'll regret it forever. And he'll come to blame you in the end."

Jess realized she was staring into her bedroom wall. She shook her head and squinted at the floor. "What are you talking about?"

Kat drew a long breath as if gathering her thoughts. Jess could almost see her in her own house staring at the ceiling, picking her words with the utmost care. "Chris is about to do something … wonderful. It will change his life forever and make him a better man than he could ever be without this opportunity. My father didn't get this chance. And he kept my mother from the experience as well. I've seen the results. You *can't* get in Chris's way."

Her voice a whisper, Jess said, "What makes you think that I'd *ever* get in Chris's way?"

"You're Catholic."

"That puts me in his way?"

"No," said Kat. "Just listen to me for a second okay?"

Again, it was the sincerity in Kat's voice that convinced Jess to give her a few more seconds of attention. "All right."

"Do you believe in the Devil, Jess?"

"I'm Catholic. You said it."

"Well throughout scriptural history, Satan has worked hard to earn the title King of Pain and Prince of Misery. He wants us all to be unhappy."

Oh, this again. Jess rubbed her eyes. "Are you saying I work for the Devil now?"

"I'm saying he might be using you, and you might not even know it." Kat waited a second, then added, "Because you have no idea what's going on."

"I *would* if someone told me." Jess grabbed her hair-brush and sat on her bed. Looking into the full-length mirror, she started working through the brown hair to which she had added so much blonde. It was a way of meditating, of thinking things through.

And she had lots of thoughts.

So many secrets murmured around her. Not even Chris felt he could tell her the truth, it seemed.

"Because no one's told me a thing," she said before she realized it.

"I wouldn't let anyone," said Kat. "That's my fault. I've been the mastermind in the background trying to bring about what is *right*."

"You? *No, it has to be bigger than you, Kat. You don't control these guys, even if you want to. And I know you don't control Tam, and certainly not Ben, even if he* hoped *you'd give it a try.*

"I was … so sure Chris wouldn't make a move," said Kat. "I thought, you know, Time heals all wounds. That this would all blow over once Chris—"

An old husky voice cut through. "Jessica?"

"Daddy?!" *When had he picked up the phone?* Her father had *never* invaded her privacy like this, before tonight.

Kat went dead silent.

"Who are you talking to?" said the old man.

"Katrina Martinez," said Jess, "from school."

"Is she a Mormon too?" he said.

Jess didn't know how much he'd heard. He enjoyed testing her obedience at times, it seemed. "What does that have to do with anything?"

"Well, hey!" said Kat, all jovial and Molly Mormon again. "It's been fun talking to you. I need to get going anyway. Nails! You know."

Oh, you're only going to make things worse, thought Jess as she shut her eyes.

"Would you come down here, please?" said her dad with genuine pain in his voice.

"Yeah. Sure, Daddy," said Jess. "Talk to you later, Kat?"

"Okay then!" said Kat. She sounded like the happiest young lady on the planet.

But Jess knew the truth. No one was happy anymore.

Chapter Twenty-One

The next morning, Chris went downstairs to have breakfast with his parents.

His mother looked at his father. They both turned eyes on him, and she said, "Chris. What's wrong?"

He held the refrigerator door open with one hand and a carton of apple juice in the other. "Why should anything be wrong?"

"It's Saturday," said Chris's father.

He carried the juice to the counter, removed a small glass from the cupboard hung at eye level, and poured up to the brim. "So?"

"It's morning," said his mother.

He grinned as they both gazed at the clock. "Ha, ha."

Four knocks erupted from the glass door that led into the backyard.

Dave stood outside with one hand shoved into the pocket of his letterman's jacket.

"Oh my!" said Chris's mother.

"It must be the end of the world," her father said. "All the teenage boys are awake before 9:00 am!"

Chris opened the door.

Dave leaned inside. "Morning Brother Noble, Sister Noble." He waved and grinned with his mouth, but not his eyes. "Your doorbell's busted."

"Make yourself at home!" said Chris's dad.

"Let's go," Dave said to Chris.

Chris looked at the small dining room table, just large enough for a family of three. "I was going to eat breakfast."

"We need to talk." Dave jerked his head to the backyard. "I'll buy."

"You never have money," said Chris, following him out.

"In that case, you buy."

"Hang on." Chris stepped inside again.

The television in the other room blurted, "Good news at last! The storm has passed. We are looking at clear skies all day, blue at the beaches, and a wonderful sunny Sunday tomorrow."

"Is it all right if I—"

Chris's father waved him away. "Go ahead."

"Take a jacket!" said his mother.

"But the weatherman just said … "

She smiled. "Trust me!"

He went into the living room, pulled on the black leather, and slipped out the glass door again. "I'll be back."

Outside, it was pouring.

From the safety of the back awning, Dave and Chris looked at the sky.

Chris shook his head.

Dave said, "I guess the weatherman doesn't have a window."

They went to Dave's truck. Chris had to jump in, Dave took off so fast. "What are you doing here, Dave."

"What. I can't take my best friend to breakfast?"

"Sounds like a fishhook if I've ever seen one." Chris knew well enough that this had something to do with Jess, though he had no idea precisely what. Dave, after all, wasn't Kat. And when it came to members of the church, Dave tended to look the other way. *Live and let live.* "Your sister put you up to this?"

"Kat doesn't control me."

"Well I'm sure she tries."

"She has questions," Dave said, sliding the truck a little through a frothing gutter as he made a left onto Buena Vista. "She thought you would have blown Jess off by now."

"What do you care," said Chris to the passenger window.

"Dude. You're my main dude! I *care*." Dave gave him a hard glance. He shook his head. "Look. I just want you to be happy. Whatever makes you happy, I got your back, okay?"

"All right." Chris stared at his feet. "I guess I've been expecting a few accusations from somebody."

"Don't worry about that," Dave laughed a little and turned another corner. "Everyone's been protecting you."

Chris stared at the side of his best friend's giant head. "Everyone?"

"You know. Tam, Kat … me …."

Chris scowled and looked away. "I don't need any protection. It's not like I'm America's secret weapon about to be unleashed upon the enemy."

"But aren't you?" Dave pulled into a parking lot before asking his next question. "Denny's?" He squealed to a stop.

"Hey, this is a truck, Dave, not a dirt bike."

Dave smiled at him. "So … you cool?"

Chris turned his hands over and examined them for Jess's invisible fingerprints. When he thought about it hard enough, he still remembered her touch, her warmth. "I don't know, Dave."

His friend nodded and popped the door open. "Honest answer. I can live with that. Let's eat, I'm starving."

As Chris slid from the truck, he touched the pockets of his jacket and his pants. "Oh. I forgot my wallet."

"Doesn't matter," said Dave. "I'll buy."

"When did you get a job?"

"One of my mother's friends." He shook one loose hand in the air. "Super hottie—she works here. You'll see."

"Did she promise to give you free food or something?" said Chris, as Dave opened both double doors at the same time and walked in like the owner of the joint.

He leaned back as Chris followed. Raising his eyebrows, he whispered, "She hit on me!"

"Oh, Dave."

"There she is," he said, barely loud enough to hear.

The woman who approached in the short green outfit opened her mouth wide. "David?!"

Dave glanced back at Chris and gave a wink.

Chris didn't smile.

The woman had to be thirty-five at least, and a mother of one on top of that.

"You *came!*" she said and grabbed Dave's shoulder.

"You said *anytime*," said Dave, offering a shy smile. "But I forgot my wallet."

"Never you mind!" Her eyes extra wide, she looked at Chris.

"Georgia, this is Chris. He's kind of my best friend."

She bit her tongue. "*Pleasure* to meet you! Come on, guys, let me find you a table where I can drool at you from the kitchen."

As they walked behind her down the aisle, Chris leaned on Dave's shoulder and mumbled, "She doesn't beat around the bush, does she."

"Just think *Free Breakfast*, Chris."

They ordered double portions of everything, and Georgia didn't even flinch. Before entering the kitchen, she peeked back at them both.

"I don't think we should have come here," Chris said.

"Don't worry. If she bites, I take the hit. You can get away scot-free."

"Leave you to get blood sucked by that vampire? What sort of friend would I be then?" Chris sipped at the water that a short woman left without a sound.

"So, are you still Peter Priesthood now?" Dave said the words without looking up from the table—as if his own water was so good, he had to savor it.

Chris licked the bit of glass in his mouth. "You think something *happened* between Jess and I? Come on, Dave."

Dave gazed out the window as the rain fell harder than it had all week. At the beginning of a "bright new day", neither of them could see the far side of the street because of the storm. "If nothing happened, say nothing happened. Or don't say nothin' at all. I don't care. I told you I got your back."

But nothing DID happen, Chris said in his mind. *Nothing but her lips on mine, my lips on hers, a lot of hand holding, snuggling close together against the cold of night, and … and the I love you part.*

Without looking across the table, Dave nodded. "Guess I got my answer."

"I didn't say—"

"I'm serious, Chris." Dave made a gesture to stop his friend from saying more. "You don't have to tell me anything. I don't need to know. I'm your friend. It's just that … I've always looked up to you."

Chris rolled his eyes left and right. Then he hung his head and sighed.

"I mean, I still do." Dave scratched his shoulder, as if

nothing special was going on. He drilled Chris in the eye. "I just wondered what you're planning on doing now?"

Leaning against the table, Chris thought, *So if I leave the church, you leave? Is that what you're saying?* "My plans haven't changed, Dave."

"Well you got that look on your face." Dave licked his bottom lip. "I saw it last night."

"What look?" Chris said, but he wouldn't make eye contact with Dave now.

"Something's going down." Dave started nodding again.

He tried not to speak. He shot his eyes around the restaurant. He didn't want to look at Dave. Best friends had a way of reading one's mind. And when he finally did, he couldn't stop the tears from adding a little extra glaze to whatever Dave was going to see.

Still as a photograph, Dave waited.

Rocking his head back and forth, Chris felt himself cracking inside. His mouth slipped open. He tried to hold back the emotions. He kept the tears at bay—that wouldn't have been cool. His voice betrayed him. "I … love her."

Dave grinned, and his eyes lit up a little. "You didn't have to tell me that part. I've known you had feelings for her for years. But like my sister, you never made a move. I don't care about that."

"Then what are you asking me?"

"When were you going to spill it about Professor Cooper?"

The name shook Chris to the bone. "What?"

Resting his hands on the table and entwining his fingers, Dave said, "Diamond Cooper. You know old Diamond Slick from his witch-hunting days?"

Chris swallowed and glanced around. "What about him."

"He's not here. I lost him on the way." Dave shrugged. "At least, I think I did."

"What are you talking about, Dave?" Chris sat upright. He hardened his eyes and turned them out the window.

"Like you don't know. Tam called me last night, but that's not the worst of it."

Chris leaned back as Georgia set their food in front of them. "Tam?"

"Here you go, boys," she said, bending forward in an immodest manner.

Dave held onto Chris's eyes for support, though Chris was too busy worrying about what Professor Cooper had to do with Tamara Cline. "That was fast," Dave said when she stood upright.

"I aim to please," she said with a flicker of sauce in her voice.

"I have no doubt about that," Dave said. He turned a serious face back to Chris, telling her with body language that this wasn't the best time to insinuate herself into their little private powwow.

"Okay," she said with a perpetual grin in her voice. "If you need me, I'll be hiding over there where I can spy on you both. Be sure to tip your waitress."

They didn't say anything else to her, but let her slink away.

"What does Tam have to do with Cooper?" said Chris with a demanding tone.

"Forget about that," said Dave. "Why did Cooper have your place staked out this morning."

"What?" Chris squinted.

Dave cocked his head to one side. "Telephoto lens in the car parked across the street. I guess he was counting on the wisdom of the weather man."

Chris looked at the front door of the glass building. He scanned the road. "What was he driving?"

"I said I lost him, didn't I?" Dave sagged into his seat. "When I got to your house this morning, all I wanted to know about was how safe you felt ... if you needed a little muscle help. Or if you wanted me to do anything with Jess."

Digging into eggs and bacon, Chris said nothing more.

"Now I'm wondering how lost you might be." Dave sighed, his final words mostly for himself: "And I'm worried I might not have the strength to help."

Chapter Twenty-Two

"That better not be one of your Mormon friends," said Mr. Singer that evening.

"Dad," said Jess, hanging her head backwards. "My friends have *always* been Mormons."

"Well not this Chris fellow." His wheelchair squeaked as he rolled slightly out of the kitchen. "You are going to mass tonight, aren't you?"

She held onto the doorknob and shut her eyes. "I promised you, didn't I?"

"And you wouldn't break your father's heart by forgetting your word, would you?"

With a loud sigh, she turned on him. "Have a *little* faith in your daughter? Please?"

He gave a small smile and rolled away, but he hadn't really looked all that appeased.

She pulled the door open.

"Jess?" said the voice outside.

She glanced around for her father. Though his ears had been failing these last few years, he would be listening as much as possible. Then she stepped onto the front porch. "What are you *doing* here?!"

Tamara Cline peeked over her shoulder. "Can't we talk?"

"Why didn't you call me?" Jess realized she had dropped to whispering. That would only be fishy. She could already hear her father's wheelchair creaking in a circle. He would appear any moment.

"We need to talk. I can't carry this weight anymore."

Jess's mouth fell open.

She's going to tell me?

"Okay," she said. "Give me a sec. How did you get here?"

"Mom's car," said Tam.

"Meet you there in a moment. Start the engine!" Jess shut the door on her friend and spun around with a great fake smile stretched across her face.

Mr. Singer appeared around the corner from the kitchen.

"You won't believe who has come to take me to mass," she said with hands raised in excitement.

"You're right. I won't believe you."

"Oh, *Daddy*!" Jess rushed by him and pecking him with a kiss on the cheek without meeting his scrutinizing gaze. "I need a pullover or something. It's still raining."

She sprinted to her room, tripped on her own feet, caught herself in the bathroom doorway, grabbed a small white sweater, and thundered down the stairs.

At the door, she froze at her father's command: "Wait!"

The hand holding the snow-colored knit tightened into a fist. Her breath locked in her lungs. She shut her eyes, opened them, and turned her grimace into a smile. When she turned, she did her best to sigh with exasperation and said with a frog in her throat, "Yeah, Daddy?"

He pointed to a squat umbrella wrapped tight with a black Velcro strap. "Don't forget this."

She laughed. "Of course!"

"I want you to make a good impression with that *Catholic* boy."

He knows, she said to herself. He knows I'm lying. Or he suspects something. I'm a terrible actress. Or maybe he's just making a point. I can't tell.

"Sure," she said, then wondered why. She had taken the umbrella. She stood a little too quiet with her back pressed against the front door.

He pointed a thick finger in the direction of the driveway. "Well get going, Jessica! You never know what the night will hold."

"Right," she said.

"But we can always wonder," he said, relaxing with a groan into his chair. "You're a tad too early for mass, of course."

"Am I?" she said, planning to look at the clock. But she had locked eyes with him unintentionally, and now she couldn't pull away.

"Dinner?" he said, raising his graying eyebrows.

With a grin she said, "I sure hope so." She opened

the door before she could drop any more clues for him to study. "I'm starving!"

She went onto the porch, then stopped again.

He was looking at her, but with the wall and the hedge in the way, he could never see the driveway, even if he tried to reposition his chair closer to the front window. Only when the car hit the street might he squint through the glass to see if Ryan was with her. With any luck, her father wouldn't remember what Ryan drove when she had dated him or when he came over on Valentine's Day.

"You going to be all right for dinner?" she said, looking back at him.

"Thought I'd do canned salmon and rice."

She slid her eyelids shut and sighed with great anguish. "Daddy, you always eat that—that or hot dogs. You want me to cook you something? I could get back early?"

He pointed his stubby finger again. "You're not my wife, young lady. I can take care of myself. Now get out there and make me a proud papa."

Did he really think she was going out with Ryan?

"What is *that* supposed to mean?!" she said with wide eyes.

He smiled.

* * *

Jess gasped when she saw the car. The passenger door waited ajar for her.

"Get in," said Tam. She revved the engine.

They pulled onto the street.

Now is when my father will get a glimpse of the car. What in the world is he going to think?

"This is *not* your mother's car, Tam!" Jess yelled as they bolted. Her back smashed so tightly into the black leather seats, she said to herself, so *this* is how an astronaut feels when leaving the Earth's gravitational pull.

Tam laughed and slapped the steering wheel. "Nope!"

"What *is* it?! And *what* are you doing with it?!"

"Remember the boy who lives next door to me?" said Tam.

"The one who got accepted to Stanford last year?"

Tam nodded. "Jeff Davies," she said. "*Still* has the hots for me."

"Oh my gosh."

"He's home for the weekend. He brought *this*." Skidding to a halt at the stop sign, she looked both ways and gunned it.

They launched together, screaming, through the intersection.

"Don't do that; I'm going to throw up!" Jess said, but she had a smile on her face. If it had been any boy driving, she would have shook her head in disdain and asked him if he thought all the macho garbage *impressed* a girl.

But since Tam was driving, it was hard not to have a good time.

"How did you get this car!" Jess yelled.

"You know, Jess. Puppy-dog eyes," Tam laughed again. "I told him all our cars were out of order and begged him to let me drive it around the block."

"You promised to go out with him," said Jess.

"No!" Then she cocked her head left. "Well, I told him he could take me for a walk on the beach after."

"The *beach*?!" Jess gawked. "Tam, it will be freezing!"

Tam slid sly eyes Jess's way. "Why do you think he said yes?"

"I don't believe this."

"I know. I have to concentrate to keep it under the speed limit. I don't even know if the registration is in the glove compartment." Tam stuck her tongue out at the rearview mirror as if someone was there.

"Jeff was in high school just last year! What is this thing? It looks like a spaceship."

"A Viper something-or-other. I don't know cars, Jess! Look in the back seat."

Jess spun around and saw, other than leather uphol-stery and fancy gizmos in the doors, absolutely nothing. Except for a paperback book. She snatched it when his name, in blue neon letters, jumped out at her. "*The Human Agent.* He *wrote* this?!?"

"He *published* it," Tam said with a finger in the air. She rested her hand on the steering wheel, made another fancy turn, and sped to the speed limit again. "Remember all that writing he used to do?"

"I don't believe it." The car stopped in a parking lot.

Jess looked up at the sign glowing blue and yellow. "No. No way, Tam. I can't come here *three times in a row!*"

"You are so funny." Tam opened the door. "Come on. My tab. All the drinks you want."

They entered Blaine's Burger, a place which had not only appeared in Jess's dreams the past two nights, but triggered emotions of emptiness and devastation, confusion and betrayal from Thursday's adventure with the missionaries in the ditch, longing and helplessness from her dinner the previous night when she was trapped in Chris's eyes.

And all day since those trials, she had attempted to dissociate herself from Chris, no matter how much her father's squinting eyes reminded her that the face interrupting her thoughts every three seconds was the face of a Mormon.

Inside the tight restaurant, Tam said, "We need to talk."

"I know," said Jess. She had already told Tam about her experience with Chris last night before Kat phoned. Tam had sat still and listened without even acknowledging that she was on the other end of the telephone. When Jess had run out of words, she had said her father needed help fetching something out of a cupboard, and that had been the end of it.

She knew Tam would need to talk this through later. She also hoped Tam might provide a few answers, and now, *finally*, it looked like Jess would get them.

"Hey, Francisco," Tam said to the guy next to the cash

register. "Could we have two Sprites?"

"I'll wait for you over here," said Jess. She stopped in front of the table where she had sat with Chris last night.

Before she could find another seat, Tam appeared behind her and said, "This looks best. It's the most private spot in the place."

"Yeah," Jess said and swallowed. "It is."

They sat, and Jess stared at the tabletop where her hands and Chris's had met and stayed. He and Jess hadn't even really eaten anything until getting into the car. It had been a booth of butterflies-in-her-stomach, and the memory of the feeling started the little beautiful wing flapping again in her gut.

"What." Tam tried to read her mind. It didn't work.

"Chris and I … came here last night."

Tam grinned, but kept serious. "You are so *fast*."

Jess pushed a few strands of hair over her right ear. "Well that sounds insulting."

"No. No, don't think that," said Tam. "I mean … people who end up getting married sometimes do this. Like you and Chris, they've known each other for, like, forever. And then, when the time is right, they jump right up to the most intense part of their relationship and wed!"

"Tam," said Jess, her eyes fluttering down as she offered a polite smile and spoke with a soft voice, "I'm still in high school."

Tam arched her eyebrows. "That's not the half of it. *Your* relationship is more complicated than you could *ever* guess."

Jess sipped her drink. "I had a feeling."

With both hands, Tam caught Jess's wrist. "It's going to be all right."

"I know," said Jess, shivering deep down. Because … it *wasn't* going to be all right. He was Mormon; she was Catholic; an apple and an orange, and they couldn't *applorange*, because there wasn't such a word!

"No, you don't know." Tam straightened. Her eyes glimmered.

Jess squinted. She turned her head to the right, but didn't release Tam from her gaze. "I know that look, Tam. What … are you thinking … young lady."

Tam bent her head forward. "Ground rules."

"Sorry?"

Tam glowed. "I've thought everything through, and I'm not bothered anymore!"

"Well," said Jess. "Wow." She shook her head as she spoke. "I am … so happy for you."

Tam slapped her wrist. "Oh, stop it and listen!"

Jess lifted her hands. She couldn't help but be hopeful, but nothing was making sense so far. "I'm listening!"

"So," said Tam. "You love him?"

"Yes." Jess blinked. *That came out WAY too fast.*

"He loves you?" said Tam.

Jess nodded her head. "I don't think his eyes can lie."

"Of course he loves you," said Tam, totally relaxed. "Now everything will go smoothly—"

"Kat called me last night."

Tam's countenance flinched. "Kat? What did she want?"

"She ... basically threatened me."

"What?!!"

Using her hand as an eraser, she wiped it once through the air. "Okay, threaten is the wrong word."

"She told you to stay away from Chris," said Tam, nodding. "That witch."

Jess shook her head. "It doesn't matter."

"You're right," Tam said, lit up again. "It doesn't. Not even Kat can get in your way if you do *exactly* as I say. You don't have much time."

"With Chris?" said Jess.

"Are you dating someone else?"

"Tam, don't do this to me." Jess put her hands to her mouth. "These past few days have been so ... hard for me. I ... get mad at myself for falling in love with someone—"

"Oh, stop it!" said Tam. "Just listen."

The blow shocked Jess first into confusion, and then uplifted her again with a fiery hope that sprang from Tam's contagious intensity.

"When do you want to lose Chris?" Tam said.

"Sorry?!?" Jess caught her lip on the straw and forgot to drink.

"Today? Tomorrow? Or do you want to get everything out of this relationship that you possibly can while you can?"

Jess had been shaking her head. She started nodding, but it ended up a quirking bobbing action to the left and to the right.

"Then you do exactly what I say!" said Tam.

"Okay!" said Jess. "Okay, Tam. I'll do it. I'll do anything. I can't eat at all anymore, girl. I can't sleep! And when I do, I dream of Chris. Chris holding me. Chris touching my fingers. Chris, Chris, Chris! It's driving me insane!"

"I know," said Tam.

Her voice cracked as her rambling continued without even a pause to listen to her friend. "Kat's trying to keep me away. I have had a billion questions—so many I don't know what they all are anymore; I should have written them down. My ex-boyfriend wants me back. Rita Hirsch wants Chris back. Some Mormon-hating professor is after Chris. And my father doesn't want me to have anything to do with an LDS boy."

She collapsed into her hands.

"And it will all wash over your back, girl," said Tam.

She gave Jess a moment to get it together.

"All right," said Jess. "What are the ground rules."

"First," said Tam, "don't ever leave him alone, and don't say no to him."

"What?!" said Jess.

"I'm kidding!" said Tam. She took a moment to laugh at the strength of the words while Jess sipped her drink. Then she said, "But, Jess, your time with him is going to be more precious than fine gold."

Jess's eyes glazed over as she repeated the last two words. "Fine gold." Precious ... that's right!

"Fine gold," Tam said a little more quickly. "Something my seminary teacher always says. Anyway. Rule number two."

"Two." Jess licked her lips. "Give it to me."

"No dates after 10:00 PM."

"What? Why not?" said Jess.

Tam shrugged, spoke, put her mouth on her drink. "Holy Ghost goes to bed at 10:00."

Jess scratched the tip of her nose. "Did you just say what I think you said?"

"Listen, do you want to keep him, or not?" said Tam, leaning forward. "Don't question my rules!"

"Okay!" said Jess with a grin.

"Because I'm not joking, girl," Tam said, though with that glimmer in her eye, she sure looked like she was making fun here. "If you don't follow these rules, he'll bolt. Maybe not right at that moment. But the next day, you'll think he's turned into the invisible man, because he won't be coming around anymore."

"10:00. Got it. Number three," said Jess.

"Number three." Tam leaned even closer and lowered her voice. "No french kissing."

Jess's face flushed. "Don't you think that's a little personal, Tamara Cline? I mean, can't we figure that sort of thing out ourselves?"

Like the beats of a hammer, four words thumped one by one out of Tam's mouth. "*No you may not.*"

Jess ran another hand through her hair.

"And no touchy-feely in the personal places, either," said Tam. "And no going all the way."

"Tam! I'm not that kind of girl, and you know it!" said Jess, a little too loud perhaps.

More than a few faces in the restaurant turned to see what the extra volume was about.

"Mind your own business!" said Tam, waving them away.

"I can't believe you'd say that."

"It's like this," Tam said, almost whispering again. "You and I both know that a lot of girls bring out the big hooks to keep their guy if they think they're going to lose him. If you had already graduated, you might consider moving in with him, for example."

"Lots of people do that," said Jess. "But Chris isn't—"

"They give their bodies to boys and believe that some-how they've bought his loyalty for forever, that they will someday-soon get married, and that because they sold their soul in this manner, they think they will live happily ever after."

"Yeah?" said Jess. There was a point to this. Not that Jess ever intended to do such a thing, but Tam was really cranking now.

"It never works," said Tam. "And none of that stuff will help you keep Chris either."

"I'm not doing any of that. We just … kissed."

Tam nodded. "Good. Because if you cross this intimacy line—french kissing, petting, or any other kind of sexual act—*it doesn't even matter if he seems to like it.*"

Jess blinked. "What do you mean?"

"*Afterwards,*" Tam said. She rolled her hand in the air. "An hour later, the next day, a couple days later, or whatever … Chris will realize that he has committed a sin."

Jess held her breath. She couldn't interrupt now. She wanted to hear it all.

Tam spoke slowly. "And he will leave you."

"A sin?" said Jess.

Tam clasped her friend's hands. "Jess. I know you. You are a good girl. Fill in the blanks. You follow the rules, this will play out fine. And you two can be—"

Jess waited. She lifted a hand. "Be what?"

Tam bit the side of her lip. "Happy. Together. Maybe … forever."

A smile exploded out of Jess's face. She took a moment to wipe away the tears. "I'd like that."

"Me too," Tam whispered. She drew a breath and put on a serious face again. "So you had better take a lesson from Rita Hirsch."

"Rita?! But she dresses like a—"

"Oh! You don't need to tell me," said Tam, swatting the thought away. "Chris used to like her, you know."

Jess rolled her eyes. "Trust me. Last year? *I* noticed."

"Yeah, well. It seems Rita couldn't keep her tongue in

her mouth."

"That's what happened? Are you kidding me?"

"Don't become a *regret* in Chris's life, Jess. *Don't become something he has to repent about later.* Trust you me! Chris dropped Rita like the dead weight she is, girl." Tam downed her soda."

They chewed their food for a while and stared off with dreamy eyes.

"All right," said Jess. "Will you tell me then what *papers* means?"

Tam choked on her soda. When she cleared her throat with a fit of coughing that drew the eyes of everyone in the burger shop, she fanned her smiling face and said, "Sorry! Sorry, Jess. I'm so sorry. How embarrassing!"

Jess sat back and folded her hands together.

"Um … what? Again, what did you say? Jess?"

"Papers?" said Jess. "Chris?" she added. "Secret Mormon code words?"

Tam laughed. "*What?*"

With big eyes and her best German accent, Jess lunged forward, barking, "Papers! Papers, please! Give us your *papers*! *Ve* have *vays* of making you talk! Papers!!!"

Tam's hands went wild in the air. She laughed, waved, swatted, and pushed the air as if she might thereby have the power to lower Jess's volume. "Okay, okay!"

Jess relaxed and gave her friend an innocent grin.

"You heard that Chris put in his papers!" said Tam.

The German accent came out again as Jess yelled one

more time, "Papers!!!"

"Yes, yes, well," said Tam, "that would be a good thing for you to know about. *Not*, mind you, that I think it poses any *problems*. Just a slight ... added bit of adventure in your wonderful relationship."

Jess rose from her seat. She leaned far across the table, setting her nose an inch from Tam's face. "Tell me, *now*. What is Chris's big secret?!!"

Standing beside their table with his hands in his pockets and a blue tie hanging from the collar of his white shirt, Chris said, "Tam. I think I ought to be the one to tell her."

Chapter Twenty-Three

Jess stood immediately. For a long time she stared at Tam, and it seemed to Chris that they spoke without making a single sound or facial tick.

All Chris said was, "There's a dance tonight. Not like the youth dance we went to on Valentine's Day. It's a Young Adult Dance. I was wondering if—" And he didn't say any more than that.

It was enough to cause a stir.

"I'll tell you everything," said Chris.

When Jess met his eyes and held them, he knew she would say yes.

"No more secrets," he said.

"Jess," said Tam. "Your *father*."

Jess didn't look away. "You'll tell me everything?"

"Anything you want to know." Chris drew close and took her hands. "Will you come?"

Dazed and unblinking, Jess said, "How did you find me?"

"There's only one Viper in town," said Chris. "When it goes by, everyone notices."

"Yeah, but—"

"Kat was out running."

"In the rain? There are health nuts, and then there're *cracked* nuts."

"Hmm. She saw you two go by."

Tam said, "And she told Dave?"

The answer was yes, but Chris shook his head. He felt himself falling into Jess's eyes as he had been drawn before. "I couldn't stay away from you. I couldn't … I needed to see you."

"Dave knew?" said Tam, trying to squeeze between them.

Chris was hardly aware she sat in the booth at all. Out of politeness, he tried to pay attention and answer her questions. He wasn't sure if she had said something else. And he couldn't take his eyes off of Jess.

"I told him everything," he whispered to Jess. I guess … Dave's looking out for me now. I wasn't sure I could go by your house. I called your cell phone, but it's turned off."

"It is?" said Jess without glancing at her pocket. Instead, she looked at his mouth.

"It wasn't too difficult to track the Viper after hearing which direction it was heading."

"You two go," said Tam. She smiled wide. "And have fun." Then serious again, she added, "But you remember what I told you, girl."

What did that mean?

Tam's words shook Chris enough to break his spell for the moment and turn his gaze to her. "Come on, Jess. We don't have much time."

As Chris pulled Jess away, Tam stuck the tip of her tongue out at Jess and shook her head.

Jess shushed her friend. She didn't let go of Chris's hand as they pushed through the glass door and made their way to the car Chris drove over here.

It was difficult to stop looking at her. Before Chris let her into the passenger seat, he found himself pressed close to her. With his right hand, he reached up and touched the side of her face. "Jess," he said, a whisper almost as soft as the rose-scented breeze blowing from the shop next door, "I—"

I love you, he thought. But could he say it? They had only dated for …

Well, had they dated at all? Officially?

He had been in love with her for so many years now, yet had stayed away.

Last night had been a world of magic swirling around him like music at a dance. And Jess had told him … that she loved him.

So what was he waiting for?
"Yes, Chris?" she said in her soft, almost husky voice.
"I …." He couldn't say it.
Why not?!
Because he had put his papers in.
Because the whole world kept them apart.

Because there was more, now, to tell her. More to cause separation rather than the beginning of an eternal relationship.

He just wanted to hold her, hold her forever.

Instead, he said, "Wait for me?"

She shut her eyes for a second. "What?"

He let go of her hands and ran into the flower shop.

A blonde woman with lizard skin, baked for years on a sunny beach, grinned at him as he skidded to a halt before the counter. "Hey, cutie," she said.

With wide eyes, Chris scanned the glass cases behind her. "I need a red rose."

"Really?" she said with a wide smile and jump of her eyebrows. "Who for."

He spoke with a soft voice. He fired off the words quick and glanced through the smoky windows at Jess leaning on his mother's Prius. "I need the flower in twenty seconds or no sale."

"Coming right up!" said the woman. She spun around, forced a sliding door open, and pulled a long-stemmed red rose from a vase of two dozen others. "Baby's breath?"

"Sorry?" said Chris, blinking and about to spring out the door.

I shouldn't have left Jess like that, he thought.

"You want me to wrap it up for you?" said the older woman.

He shook his head and took it from her fingers so fast, a thorn almost tore her skin. "How much?"

"Hey!" she said, babying her hand and scowling. "$3.50 for you, honey."

Throwing a five-dollar bill on the counter, he ran out the door.

"Here," he said, bringing the rose up between his face and Jess as he pressed close.

She smiled. "Chris, I—"

"No," he said. "I'm the one who has cheated you."

"Cheated?" she said.

He touched her lips with one finger. "By not talking to you. By holding back."

"Well," she said, sniffing the rose. "You *are* a man of few words."

"But I shouldn't be," he said. "Not with you, Jess." Close enough to sniff the rose himself, he bent forward to do so."

Jess must have thought he was moving in for a kiss. Up she went on her toes. Her mouth closed against his.

And he kissed her.

"Ap!" said Tam, exiting Blaine's Burger. She waved a hand in the air and slapped her hip. "Don't mind me. I'm just … going back to the car. Not here. Please continue, whatever it was I didn't see you doing."

Chris and Jess watched Tam climb into the black Viper and start the engine. Tam wore the silliest look on her face, as if *she* had been the one caught kissing.

She waved again, acted like she wasn't watching them, and glanced at them repeatedly until she fired the Viper out of the parking lot with a roar.

Jess looked at the sky. "Hey!"

"What is it?" said Chris looking into the heavy rolls of clouds floating east, at the blue beyond, and the red and orange glow of the end of day.

"It stopped raining," she said looking back at Chris's eyes and lips. "The storm is over."

Yes, thought Chris as he studied the sky again. *Oh, I wish that was only true. But one thing is for sure.* "The sun is coming out," he said to Jess. "It will be bright. At least … for a little while."

Chapter Twenty-Four

On the way to the dance, Chris avoided whatever it was that he really wanted to say. He explained that the Valentine's Day Dance had been what members of the Church of Jesus Christ of Latter-day Saints call a Youth dance, and that normally they were held on Fridays, and that normally you didn't sneak in the back door, but she hadn't had a dance card and Tam thought the whole thing would be fun, and Chris … well it was one of Chris's regrets to be so dishonest.

It was the regret part that bothered Jess.

Wasn't this what Tam had warned her about? So Jess had to ask. "You regret going to that dance … with me … then?"

Chris looked at her with wide eyes. "Are you kidding?"

She didn't know what that meant. Inside, Jess crossed her heart and hoped to die before ever doing anything with Chris that he might regret later for religious reasons.

And she did everything to avoid thinking about her father.

She was supposed to be at mass right now.

No! I'm not going to think about it.

Her father would ask her later what the priest had talked about. For that reason, she wished they still did mass in Latin. Then she could just shrug her shoulders and tell her father she didn't know, but that it had been a great, spiritual experience, and that she felt at peace for going.

Stop it! she said in her mind, trying to regain control. *Listen to Chris. Don't think. Just listen!*

Of course, that was a ludicrous thing to command herself to do. It was like saying, *Don't breathe, even if you have to. Just don't.*

Chris went on, talking about how LDS kids from ages fourteen to eighteen went to these Youth dances that required dance cards passed out by the local Mormon bishops. From age nineteen on, members of the Church went to what was called Young Single Adult dances.

"But I just turned eighteen, Chris," Jess said with the utmost caution. She focused hard on his countenance, trying to read his thoughts.

He stared straight ahead, so she couldn't see a thing in his mind.

Tam's voice ricocheted off the insides of her brain: *Don't become something he has to repent about later.*

"Chris," she said.

"Yeah?"

"Maybe we shouldn't go to the dance."

His head swiveled slowly on his neck. He looked into her eyes for as long as he could before he had to gaze back at the road. "You don't … want to go with me to the—"

"Slacks and a long sleeve shirt?" she said. "I'm not really dressed for it."

"I think you … you look beautiful." He cleared his throat and tried to aim his eyes forward again. "Besides. I hear these YSA dances are different. The dress standards aren't so harsh. And they don't require dance cards."

After hesitating for a moment, Jess touched his forearm. "I don't want to get you in any trouble," she said, though those hadn't been the words she'd intended.

He smiled and shook his head. "Trust me. You won't."

"I mean …." Jess shut her eyes.

"What," said Chris.

"I don't want you to regret going out with me."

He pulled over and turned off the engine. "Why would you think that?"

The slowing of the car and sudden silence of the engine shocked Jess. She couldn't say anything at first.

"Is it because we belong to different religions? Is it because your father wants you to *stay* Catholic? Or … did Tam tell you …."

She shook her head. "You were going to tell me. Remember?"

"Jess? Right now … there is absolutely nothing I want more than to be with you."

She opened her mouth. Not even a hiss of air came out.

He took her hand, rubbing his fingers over her knuckles and into the palm she enclosed in a loose fist. "You see," he said. Now his mouth hung open.

Jess cocked her head to the side and squinted.

Cars passed them, and one was so loud, Jess didn't bother to look but thought it might have been Tam scoping things out from her black Viper.

"Tell me, Chris," she said, her voice weak. She squeezed his fingers. "It's all right."

"I don't have much time," he said.

Oh my gosh, thought Jess.

The tears came out instantly, though she managed to suck her lips into her mouth a little and bite on them to keep them from trembling.

Chris ... is dying!

"You heard the missionaries in the hospital ask if I had put my papers in," he said.

She grabbed his arm and held it tight. "Just tell me one thing, Chris."

He put his other hand on hers. "I'm telling you everything, Jess."

"Then—"

He held up a finger. "No. Let me do it my way, all right?"

She nodded as one tear broke down her face. Then she lunged across the seats and kissed him.

Beneath her hands and her lips, Chris trembled. Heat rose, and with it, a cologne fragrance she did not know, but wanted to smell forever.

Her eyes had closed. And she clamped her teeth together to make sure nothing moved that shouldn't.

When one of her eyelids eased its way up, she could see the magic of the glowing sunset outside.

Through the driver's side window, cars blurred past her, and she could hear herself breathing with him.

Their lungs entwined, their hearts pounding together, her fingers on his face, his fingertips pressed into the clenched muscles of her arms, she saw across the street where a familiar PT Cruiser had parked.

Through the window of the roadster, she saw the large round lenses of a black camera.

A face rose beyond the camera.

Professor Diamond "Slick" Cooper smiled at her.

With the faintest hum, she removed her lips from Chris's mouth.

He helped her back to her side of the car—no, *he pushed her.*

It had been gentle, but now the look on his face was one of confusion and terror.

"We can't do that," he said, his eyes darting about the floor. "We can't kiss in the car." He seemed to be speaking to himself. "Bad things can happen when two people kiss in a parked car."

Jess put her hands to her mouth.

What have I done! she said to herself. "Take me to the dance now?"

With shaking hands, Chris started the car.

It squealed away.

When Jess took a moment to peek out the rear window, she didn't see Professor Cooper's car.

He wasn't following them.

Maybe ... he didn't need to anymore.

Chapter Twenty-Five

Jess seemed far more nervous going into the Stake Center on Colville Road this time than she had been on Valentine's Day. She kept looking up at Chris as if ready to say, *Are you* sure *this isn't a bad idea?*

Chris just couldn't believe he'd kissed her sitting down in his mother's car. That had been a big no-no he had learned from Brother Higby, his Teacher's Quorum advisor at church, many years ago.

He had broken the rule with Rita Hirsch. Soon after, she had introduced french kissing—which she just called "passionate kissing"—into their little romantic rituals.

At first, kissing like that had really surprised him. Then he started to like it, to even look forward to it. And that had lasted for weeks.

But it had been so physical, so carnal, he felt he had to avoid thinking about certain teachings, though he couldn't quite figure out which ones. He felt guilty, but he wasn't sure why. He didn't remember anyone *saying* No French Kissing! Most of his advisors had said things like, no *necking* or petting or going all the way. Some had said,

Don't kiss for longer than two seconds, or something like that. And of course, Brother Higby had said don't kiss in a parked car, but that was probably because in his generation, teens used to go park someplace at night where they could sit together and see the city lights and "make out." Now-a-days, you could just do that in the hallways of the high school.

His relationship with Rita had ended the day he read one particular scripture that had slapped him in the side of the head: "The natural man is an enemy to God ...."

It had only been a feeling in his heart, but Chris knew that kissing that way with Rita just had to be one of those things that only married people were allowed to do. He had grown to like french kissing, even though he had kept the act a secret from his parents. Part of him didn't want to stop. But he knew it was that same Natural Man part that also grew in its urges to do more things ... things Rita might have allowed, might have even wanted to do.

To become an *enemy to God*, however, was *not* what Chris hoped for. He had been reading *The Book of Mormon*. He knew it was true. And he wanted to serve a mission.

And so the relationship had ended.

He had also continued to stay away from the beautiful Catholic girl that had enchanted him all these years.

"I didn't expect to get together with you," he said as Jess and Chris stood on one side of the dance floor. It had already been a little more than two hours, and they hadn't danced yet.

Through the dim lights, blues and yellows and reds came alive, flashed around, and settled, only to start up a moment later from the DJ's little gizmo on the stage of the cultural hall.

Jess grinned, her eyes on the floor. The loud music forced them to stay close and speak up a bit. "Neither did I. But I had always hoped."

"I think I hoped too," said Chris. He stared into her eyes, waiting for the next slow song to begin. "It just seemed impossible."

"It is," said Jess.

Hot and cold blasted through Chris's face. "What do you mean."

She had a hold of both of his hands, and she glanced down at them, then back up to his face. "Look at us. I'm here. You're here." She squeezed him. "And it is impossible. But here we are."

The slow song started before Chris was ready. He had been swimming in her eyes, maybe even swaying back and forth with her, but not to the beat of whatever thunder had been playing around them a moment ago.

And he didn't remember opening his mouth, but felt it open.

"I love you, Jess."

Her eyes sparkled in the spin of lights.

The slow mood music rocked them back and forth until they really were dancing, holding each other close, and still mixing the colors of their eyes.

She smiled. She beamed. She almost cried, it seemed. "I love you, Chris." She licked her lips, thinking for a moment. Then she said, "And I'm never going to leave you."

He swallowed. He nodded. "Then I had better tell you everything."

"Okay." With soft eyes ready for the most drastic news, she stared up at him like one who would not break, no matter what he said. Her stalwart face, filled with emotion, honest love, and integrity confirmed what her mouth had said only seconds before: I am *never* going to leave you.

"Two weeks ago, I put my papers in," he said, and then ran out of breath.

She nodded, not understanding, yet waiting with the patience of a loving wife.

"Today ... I got my call."

She blinked. "You ... got what?"

With lips so dry Chris could almost hear them cracking and a tongue that could not wet them if he wanted it to, he said, "In four weeks ... I'm going on a mission ... to Japan."

Jess continued to stare into him. Inside her head, Chris could discern a brain jumping from one thought to another, calculating, analyzing, postulating, predicting, measuring, collating determinations, and seeking desperately for an answer.

He swallowed, unsure of her reaction. Thinking fast,

he glanced at the dance floor and led her into the middle of it.

She walked as if without a brain at all.

Chris took her right hand with his left and placed his right hand on the small of her back.

Her head came to rest against him.

And they danced to the music of a sad love song that promised nothing.

At the end of the song, a screech turned into a scream which then mutated into a joyous yell, the beginning of a deafening song that Jess had to shout over as they stood still. She squinted through the rapid blasts of yellow, blue, and red lights. "So this means you are leaving *me*."

He leaned his head down to speak with lower volume.

Jess took a step back.

Oh, it is *impossible*, Chris thought. But he said the words in his mind anyway: "I'll be gone two years, Jess."

She nodded at him and licked the corner of her mouth.

"It's important to me," he said.

Somehow, her hands had fallen to rest on her cocked hips. Tears built up in her eyes and spilled down her cheeks. She didn't bother to wipe them, or even to cry. She stood like a girl on the verge of a fight. Obviously, she had already been slugged in the gut. "Am *I* important to you?"

He stepped closer, bending forward again, trying to catch her hands and missing. "Yes!"

"Four weeks?" She shook her head, still licking the

corner of her mouth, desperate to hold back the powerful throws of weeping she felt mounting up inside of her. "You won't even be here when I graduate?"

He held his breath. Slowly, he shook his head.

She nodded again. Spinning around, she yanked her arm away when Chris reached out and touched it. She lifted one finger to say she needed a moment.

But she was walking, and she kept walking. And Chris couldn't see her face because she didn't want him to.

As she went out the door and into the foyer, she drew out her cell phone.

Before she made it to the outer doors, Chris caught up to her. "Jess!" The words almost came out a whine, instead of the innocent and honest plea he was trying to make.

At the glass she turned, but did not meet eyes with him at first.

He didn't know what to say.

I won't go on my mission! came to mind, but that would have been a lie. After learning that the gospel was true, not even his parents could have kept him from going forth to serve the Lord.

Wait for me! also came to mind, and that was worse than the first thought. But. A Catholic girl waiting for an Elder in the Church of Jesus Christ of Latter-day Saints to get home? For *what*?!

Jess looked at him, her eyes swollen, tears dripping from her long lashes to her chin. She couldn't sustain the anger or even the look of pain on her face. Her love for him drew more tears and opened her mouth. "Do you really love me, Chris?"

"Yes," he said.

"Are you dying?"

He jerked his head back. "No, Jess."

She smiled. "Well. I could always hope, right?"

"What?" He took a step toward her.

She lifted a hand for him to stop. "Will you give me a few minutes? I think I need some air."

He cleared his throat and put his hands into his pockets. "Take all time you need, Jess. I'll be right here. I won't leave you."

Her eyes didn't blink as she scrutinized those last few words. Then she pushed the door open and went outside.

Chris paced the foyer for a while. From time to time, he glanced at Jess, her back turned to the church, her arms wrapped around herself as she trembled in the cold. Her face pointed up to the stars shining through the broken clouds overhead.

Maybe she's praying, thought Chris.

A roar slowed and grew silent as a black Viper pulled up.

As Chris pushed the church door open, Jess slid into the passenger seat. She glanced back only once.

"Jess!"

Tam hit the gas. The Viper squealed out of the parking lot, onto Colville Road, and roared until Chris couldn't hear it anymore.

Chapter Twenty-Six

She arrived home just before midnight.

"That you, Jess?" said her father as Jess tried to close the door without a sound.

The wheelchair squeaked and rolled from the hall.

Jess let the door click shut. She turned and rested her back against it.

"How was mass, this evening?" he said with foreknowledge in his tone.

She stared at him through puffy eyes. Tam had listened. That girl could talk up a storm, but when it came to it, Tam was the best listener a friend could have. But that was all. Jess wanted someone to tell her what to do. Only … not her father. So who did that leave? Kat? Dave? Her cousin, Ben?

"I take it from your silence," Mr. Singer said, "that you didn't get much out of mass tonight."

He's leaving me, Jess thought. *That's what all the hubbub has been about. That's why there had been so much hesitation, so many secrets. Everyone knew about these "papers" going in. No one had told her, not even Tam, probably because Kat the*

Killer Mormon would have assassinated anyone who didn't let this play out.

And how WOULD it end?

Isn't it obvious?

Not only could her father have answered the question, but he was most likely going to, Jess figured.

A good Catholic girl and a good Mormon boy *will not* get together. It was as simple as that. That just wouldn't do.

They just won't.

No matter how much they love each other.

That's been Kat's big take all along. That's why Tam had to struggle to keep the papers secret, even though she wanted Jess and Chris together as much as Jess did. And Dave's been stuck in the middle, trying to be there for his best friend however he might be needed.

Why hadn't Ben said something?

He didn't know. That was it, right?

So Tam had let all these things happen because she couldn't stop it. And the peace Tam must have expected would come in the knowledge that if Chris and Jess *did* get together, even if it was only for a matter of weeks, they could still have the most romantic four weeks in the history of love. Just as if Chris had been about to die, and she as the true and last love of his life, had promised to stay with him until the very end.

Only, Jess didn't want to see it that way. Chris wasn't dying. He was leaving her.

But … he'd said he loved her.

He actually said *it.*

Jess covered her eyes. She slid down the door, landing on her bottom. She tried to hide behind her knees so her father wouldn't spot her weeping into her hand.

"Did you think I wouldn't find out?" he said with a gruff voice.

She didn't answer. It took all of her remaining strength just to keep the crying silent.

"I don't break when I see a woman cry, young lady," said her father. "Do you want to know how I found out?"

She didn't move. He could talk all he wanted. *It doesn't even matter anymore, does it?*

No. NOTHING does.

"Ryan Stokes came by when you didn't show up for communion," said her father. He waited for her to say something in defense. After all, she had told him it was *Ryan* who had come to take her out for food and then off to mass.

But it didn't matter. The whole world could melt away now. Jess wouldn't mind. All the important parts were gone or going anyway.

"Ryan said he got a call from a certain college professor from hereabouts," said her father.

Jess didn't move her hand from her eyes.

"This college professor was, he said, concerned about *my daughter*! Now, Jessica, ask me why."

She didn't.

"Because *my daughter* is dating some Mormon boy!" The wheelchair creaked forward. "Did you *think* I wouldn't find out, young lady?"

Flinging her hands and pushing off the floor, Jess said, "I don't care!!!"

She raced past him and stopped at the base of the stairs. Mr. Singer had climbed those steps a million times until his legs gave out. Now, the upstairs was her safe haven away from him. She also knew it ripped them apart. And she couldn't bear to hurt her father's feelings.

And right now, outside of a listening friend, her father was all Jess really had.

"Jessica?" her father whispered, turning the chair slowly to face her. "What's … what's happened?"

She slumped onto the steps. The tears rolled. She heaved and shuddered. And when she looked back at him, she saw her own pain reflected in his frown. She wiped her wet cheeks, but couldn't stop sobbing, even as she spoke. "He loves me, Daddy."

He waited, water in his eyes—which was not unusual, since his old eyes bothered him all the time.

"I love him," she said. She couldn't speak anymore, but pushed the words out anyway. "And … he's leaving me."

Chapter Twenty-Seven

After knocking, Chris's mother pushed his bedroom door open. "It's seven o'clock, Christopher. If you want breakfast, you'd better get down here."

Chris rolled in his bed and faced the wall.

"And remember," his mother said, "until next January, we're on the early-morning schedule. Sacrament Meeting starts at 8:00, so you'd better eat and shower right away."

As the door started to close, Chris said, "I won't be eating today."

His mother didn't make a sound. Maybe she had already left. Then her weight settled on the edge of the bed. "Chris?"

He hummed once.

"Are you fasting?"

He waited, then hummed once again.

"It's not Fast Sunday, you know," she said, her voice trembling. "Is everything all right?"

"I got my call yesterday," he said.

"What?!" She made a few short sounds in her throat.

Chris didn't turn around or rise.

"Did you … open it?"

"I didn't tell anyone. I just wasn't in the mood."

She laughed, but he heard the fear in her laughter. "You've been waiting for this all your life, Chris. How could you not be in the mood?"

"It's that Catholic girl," said his father in the door. "Jessica Singer."

There was something heavy in his voice, something wrong.

Chris leaned up and rubbed one eye.

His father frowned. He held the Sunday paper in his hand. "Seems you made the back page, boy."

His dad handed it to Chris, and Chris read the title of the article:

FUTURE MORMON MISSIONARY NOT PREPARED, BUT THAT'S OKAY!

"Professor Diamond Cooper has named you the 'Mormon to Watch' as you prepare for your mission," said Chris's father. "Why would that be?"

The picture in the bottom corner of the paper answered the question. It showed Chris in his mother's parked car the previous night before the sun had gone down. Jess was practically on top of him. He was holding her there. And it looked like Jess was devouring his face while he enjoyed every minute of it.

The caption on the tiny photograph said, NOT QUITE THE MORMON THING TO DO.

Down the hall, the telephone rang. "I'll get that," said his mother.

She disappeared as Chris stared at the picture in the paper and at the headlines.

Not angry, but certainly thinking hard, his father stared at him.

"Don't worry about this," Chris said.

When his father left the room and started whispering in the hall with Chris's mother, Chris scanned the article.

It was the regular Diamond Cooper garbage:

> Can a Mormon do this sort of thing?
>
> What ever happened to standing a little taller?
>
> Maybe Chris Noble didn't get the memo. Or maybe that's okay! Maybe Mormons are all talk and no play, and the truth is finally coming out.
>
> According to sources, he's supposed to be preparing for a mission.
>
> And what's the first thing he does?
>
> A show for all the local folks down Sunset Boulevard!
>
> He threw his hands into the air, he slapped them down on the guy—who was *supposed to be* hurt, and just happened to be a Mormon missionary, or in other words a very willing person ready to play the part of one receiving the miracle of a healing blessing—and with a whole lot of bogus chanting in the fury of a

storm, he pronounced the poor guy whole!

But then, an ambulance still had to whisk the victim away.

A doctor still had to work on the guy.

And only after a day in the hospital to make it look like things were serious, the missionary checked out and has, according to sources, gone right back to work knocking on *your* doors!

But that's not all.

No, my friends!

For the shallow price it takes a young Mormon man like Christopher Noble to purchase sin, we receive an even better surprise.

Here! See the young Mormon missionary-to-be making out on the face of an otherwise innocent Catholic girl, Jessica Singer, in the front seat of his mother's car!

Does he have any standards at all?!?

If the young men and women of Mormonism are supposed to be so special and careful as they prepare to serve missions for their church, then why is one such as Chris Noble out feasting his face on members of another apostate religion?!

What sort of example is Chris Noble setting?

Or is it all talk anyway.

I say it is—all talk! Words, words, words.

And yet not the right words!

Join us at 7:00 PM on Wednesday at the 1st Chapel of the Resurrection on Fig Street in the City of Harmon for an open discussion of the Mormon Scourge and the Example of Chris Noble on the Youth of the World.

How are we to know the wolves from the sheep in the latter days, according to our Savior?

Jesus said, "By their fruits shall ye know them!"

Join us Wednesday as we break open the fruits of Mormon kind and discover the true colors therein!

"Chris," said his mother in the doorway again. She held the telephone to her chest to muffle the noise. "It's ...."

He blinked at the paper again. He knew who was on the phone. "Jess?"

"No. It's the Stake President," she said.

He lowered the paper. "President Beals?"

Her face was pale. "He wants to meet with you this afternoon."

* * *

After Sacrament Meeting, Dave and Chris made their way to the drinking fountain.

"Oh," Chris said. "You read the paper too?"

"Are you kidding me?" said Dave. "Have you seen all the eyes on you this morning? Either your magnetic personality is drawing their attention, or everyone on the stinking planet read about you and Jess this morning."

Chris fought the urge to rub his eyes. That would only attract attention and stir a few thoughts, he figured. He kept his face emotionless and his eyes forward.

"Don't worry about Wednesday, dude," Dave said, his hands stuffed into the pockets of his slacks. Sunday at church was the only time he didn't wear his letterman jacket.

"Wednesday?" said Chris.

"Yeah. The day Diamond Slick takes you apart in front of half the City of Harmon."

"Thanks."

Dave gave him a dark grin. "Don't mention it. I'm going to go and pummel him into their little Protestant pulpit."

"Oh yeah," said Chris. "That will show people this is the true church once and for all." When they reached the drinking fountain, he had to stop himself from leaning down and sipping water. He was fasting. He had plenty of reason to fast right now.

"Well how long are we supposed to put up with all this anti-Mormon garbage?!!" Dave spoke a little too loudly and it drew plenty of eyes. "I mean, we're not living in the backwater 1800's anymore? This isn't even the 1900's! I am sick and tired of people bashing on Mormons because they don't have standards like the rest of us and we make them feel uncomfortable."

Chris met eyes with some who passed and grinned cordially. Those in the distance weren't smiling, but they sure watched all they could. "Keep your voice down."

Dave punched the water fountain and took a drink.

"Jesus said that if we are persecuted like him because we stand on his side, we'll be numbered among the prophets. They were persecuted the same way."

Snapping his large body up into a standing position again, Dave got so close to Chris's face, he wondered if Dave planned on punching him. "Well I'm *sick* of persecution. I say we go *The Book of Mormon* route. Anyone who doesn't want to follow the gospel can either keep their mouths shut or we hang 'em from a tree!"

"I don't think that's exactly what happened," said Chris.

Starting toward class, Dave said, "Whatever."

"Don't go, Dave. I'll go talk to the people."

Dave came back. "Don't even think about that, man. You go into that den of lions, and they *will* skin you alive. Not with teeth and nails, mind you, but words! Trust me."

"I have to do something," said Chris. "Cooper mentioned ... he named Jess in the article."

Pushing a finger into Chris's face, Dave said, "Don't go."

* * *

"Brother Noble," said President Beals, shaking Chris's hand and gripping his shoulder at the same time. "Come on in. Thanks for seeing me today. And congratulations on your call!"

"Thank you, President," said Chris. "How did you

find out about it?"

"Your bishop phoned me after your meetings this morning. Japan, wasn't it?"

President Beals shut the door. He lifted a hand. "Please. Have a seat."

"Sapporo." Chris sat in one of the two green padded chairs as the Stake President walked around his desk and sat in front of a large window.

"Ah! The *Frozen Chosen*!" He laughed with a gentle voice. "Get a good coat. You'll be very far north. When do you report to the Missionary Training Center?"

"Four weeks," said Chris. He wondered why his voice was so scratchy.

"Wonderful. May I say a little prayer?"

President Beals never ceased to amaze Chris. The power of the priesthood weighed heavily on the man, and his devotion to the Lord was clear. At all times and in all places, one could see love, personal interest in others, and concern in his eyes. More than any other man Chris had known, President Beals bore the burdens of others and mourned with those who mourned.

And now he was asking *Chris* if it was okay to say a little prayer.

"Of course," Chris said. He clasped his hands together and bowed his head.

"Father in Heaven," said President Beals. "We thank thee for our many blessing and our wonderful opportunities to serve thee in this life. We pray at this time that thy

Spirit may attend us. Help us to remember thy blessings and the sacrifice of thy Son as we worship thee this day."

Through all that had happened to Chris, his testimony had remained strong. He'd learned through the power of the Holy Ghost and through fervent study and prayer that the Church was true. He had come to a realization that the Savior was *his* Savior. God loved him, and sent His son, that if Chris might follow Jesus Christ, he might find everlasting happiness in the eternal worlds to come.

When the Stake President said *Amen*, it started Chris out of a fuzzy vision. He remembered his testimony and the wonderful days that followed his learning of the true meaning of the gospel.

"Amen!" he said.

And President Beals smiled across the desk.

Unsure of what to say or do, Chris took a moment to look at the giant painting on the wall.

In the picture, a new rendition of a famous scriptural scene, Jesus Christ knelt in the garden of Gethsemane. With His hands clasped together and resting against a large boulder, the Son of God turned His eyes heavenward, and they seemed to say, *Abba* ... Daddy ... please take this cup from me. Nevertheless, let not *my* will be done ... but *thine* ....

"I love that painting," said the President, having followed his gaze. He took a slow deep breath with his mouth and blew it out through his nostrils. "It reminds me how *alone* Jesus was as he passed through more pain and suffering … and loneliness … than I can ever imagine."

"Our older brother," said Chris. It was a testimony of a sort, an agreement with what the Stake President had said. Otherwise, Chris was still filling the silence. He didn't know what to do.

"Have you ever felt alone, Brother Noble?"

"Often," said Chris.

"Well, it won't be that way on your mission. Every morning you'll wake up and see your companion's face. Over breakfast, same face. All day long, every meal, and even when you go to sleep at night, same, same, same face. And you'll meet a thousand people. The field is white."

"D&C 4," said Chris, recognizing the words.

"The missionary section!" said President Beals. "You've been studying. That's wonderful."

"Thank you." Chris shifted in his seat. When would the President mention the newspaper? When would he ask about Jess? Now? Surely those were the reasons why he had been called into this special interview. He had already done everything required to serve a mission. And in all honesty, he wanted to press forward for the Lord, with all his heart, might, mind, and strength.

But with Chris in the public eye like this, well … in a way, Chris represented the Church.

He looked at the painting on the wall. In that special garden, Jesus Christ took upon him all the burdens of the world. Heavenly Father placed on his shoulders more pain and pressure than Chris could ever handle. He suffered for everyone.

I'm not as strong, Chris thought. *I can't represent everything.*

And yet, came a thought to his mind, *You will represent me in the mission field.*

"There's a scripture I would like to share with you, Brother Noble." The president lifted his large-print Bible and set it aside. He hefted his triple and said, "I see you have the *Doctrine and Covenants* with you?"

"Yes, here." Chris opened his quad to the D&C.

"Section 121, then."

Chris flipped the pages as fast as he could.

"Look here in verse 34," said President Beals, as he slipped on his bifocals. "There are *many called*, but *few are chosen* … why …?" He looked up.

While this sounded quite familiar, Chris didn't remember reading any of this section before. Maybe because it was so deep in the D&C. He decided to admit his ignorance by shaking his head.

The President grinned and gazed back into his scriptures. "The next verse says it is because they fail to learn a lesson for two different reasons. Both are mentioned in 35, but I think I know you, and I know you do not aspire at this point to the honors of men, so we'll just look at the first reason."

"Okay," said Chris, and he wondered if he should have said Thank you instead. He looked at the scripture, following along as the Stake President read aloud.

"There are many called, but few are chosen … *because their hearts are set so much upon the things of this world* …." He removed his glasses and smiled with sincerity at Chris once more.

Chris swallowed and thought, I'll have to get a looser collar on my mission shirts, because this one is killing me.

"You have a girlfriend?" said President Beals.

Opening his mouth to say no, Chris said, "Yes."

"That's wonderful," said the President. His eyes glowed and his face softened so much, Chris knew he really meant it. There was no sarcasm in the words. "And what is her name?"

Chris's voice came out hoarse. "Jessica Singer."

"Jessica … a lovely name. Now tell me, Chris. You are one of the called. But are you also one of the few who are chosen?"

Wetness built in the back of Chris's nostrils. A lump of emotion filled his throat. "President Beals?"

The President gave a nod.

"I *know* that God lives. He has told me so. And I am *so thankful* for Jesus Christ, that I *will* go forth with all my heart, and all my mind, and with all my might, and with all my strength." A tear dropped down the front of his face. "I will serve the Lord."

President Beals sat still for a moment. He leaned back in his chair, resting one hand on his triple combination after closing the book.

It occurred to Chris that the President had the power

to stop him from going on a mission. The thought was a hammer that hit his heart with such a thud that it seemed to stop with a jolt and start up again.

A great peace covered President Beals's face. "I have no doubt, Brother Noble, that you will be a wonderful missionary. Thank you for meeting with me today."

"Thank you," said Chris, relieved. As he began to rise, the Stake President lifted a hand.

"Chris? Will you give a word of prayer as we part?"

"Sure."

President Beals came around the large desk and knelt beside the twin chairs, and Chris knelt with him.

Chris folded his arms and closed his eyes, unable to rid himself of the painted image of Jesus' imploring face on the Mount of Olives. *Not my will be done*, said the eyes of the Savior in his mind, *but thine.*

He opened his mouth to pray. And he cried.

Chapter Twenty-Eight

The whole week had been a blur, so far, and Jess still knew very little.

Her father hadn't seen Professor Cooper's article in the Sunday paper until Jess pointed it out. Then he stewed on the porch for a few hours while Jess contemplated painting her toenails, which she hadn't done in a few years, or doing her homework, which she had otherwise forgotten about since her Thursday night date with Chris, Tam, and the Hulk Meister.

Before she could finish her pre-calculus at the kitchen table, her father rolled in with the newspaper on his lap and said three words, "This is wrong."

* * *

On Monday, Chris had the audacity—or bravado—to come to her house.

But Tam had driven Jess to her house rather than home, so Jess's father opened the door. Evidently, Chris had stayed quite a while.

That night, Jess mustered the strength to call him, though she didn't have a clue what she would say. Saturday night at the dance had kind of knocked the wind out of her. She still loved him, though with only four weeks before he left her, she didn't know what to do with those emotions.

When he came on the phone, he said it was Family Night. Actually, he said he was in the middle of Family Home Evening, or something like that. It didn't make much sense to her, but the point was plain. He couldn't talk. He would call her tomorrow. She said that would be fine.

* * *

On Tuesday, at school, Jess bumped into Kat in the hallway. Kat only said one thing. "Don't get in the way Jess."

Jess replied, "The only person I have seen in anyone's way, Kat, is you."

Kat gave her a sweet smile with poison in her eyes.

"You know Kat, you make me wonder if *you* have feelings for Chris. And if you do, you really ought to talk to him. Because no matter what is going to happen, Chris has already told me the name of the woman he's in love with. And it isn't you."

Kat turned red and looked ready to either cry or punch Jess in the kisser. A sigh eased from her throat. She smiled at Jess, then surprised her by singing a song that started something like this: "Let us all press on in the work of the Lord, that when life is o'er we may gain our reward …." She walked, no … she pranced away.

They didn't speak any more after that.

After school, Jess had Tam drive her to the Good Guys to see if Chris was working. When they didn't find him there, Tam drove her to Chris's house, where she met his parents.

They were very nice, and they called Tam 'Tamara,' and said they remembered when she was a little girl in the ward—the use of that last word made Jess wonder if they were all crazy, and if she was liable to become crazy hanging around them.

They didn't know where Chris was either, but kept Jess and Tam there for hours.

Chris's father explained that he worked at home online. His mother had never worked out of the home. When Jess asked if that was a rule in the Church of Jesus Christ of Latter-day Saints—that women are to be stay-at-home moms with no other careers—she laughed and said, "Why would I want *two* careers? Actually, after Chris leaves for Japan, I was going to apply for a position teaching the first grade, or second grade—I haven't decided which."

"Don't you need a degree for that?" Jess had asked. "And a teaching credential?"

"Of course!" Mrs. Noble had replied. Then she leaned forward and touched Jess's hand. "That women should get an education *is* a rule in our church."

Jess gained a lot of respect for Chris's mother that day. And she thought his kick-back father was the coolest.

But Chris didn't come home before Tam said she had to bail.

"Do you think he'll be back anytime soon?" Jess asked his dad.

"Well … *now* I think I know where he went." He gave his wife a look.

"Where?" Jess said, and glanced at Tam, who honestly looked dumbfounded.

Nodding to her husband, Chris's mother said, "The Temple."

"If he went there, he might stay until it closes," said Mr. Noble. "He won't be *late* until long after dark."

That night, Jess wrote letter after letter after letter, organizing her thoughts. Each letter was addressed to Chris.

She described her frustrations, her concerns, her worries. She detailed her hopes, her dreams, and the promises she was willing to make. But the confusion spun her in circles, and she vowed not to ever show those letters to anyone. Under her bed, she kept them all.

* * *

Wednesday surprised Jess with two exams she had completely forgotten about.

Thoughts of Chris Noble had become all consuming.

And today was the day Professor Diamond Cooper was speaking at the 1ˢᵗ Chapel of the Resurrection on Fig Street. The Sunday paper described "an open discussion of the Mormon Scourge and the Example of Chris Noble to the Youth of the World."

She expected Cooper to stand at a pulpit and shout rather than discuss, getting all the congregation and curious people to nod their heads and murmur words of affirmation.

No matter what happened, Jess planned on attending.

It was her picture in the paper. It was her fault—she couldn't bear the images of death and loss in her head, and she had just jumped on Chris, she loved him so much. And she had also seen Cooper taking the picture, and had said nothing to Chris.

When Professor Cooper mentioned her name, she planned to stand up and defend herself.

If her father found out about that, he could lock Jess behind doors until she moved out for good.

Tam drove Jess home that day. Jess didn't want to tell her the plan, so she didn't talk at all.

Tam rattled on for a little while about Dave. "Do you think he likes me? I mean, I don't want to be the only girl who doesn't have a guy fawning over her. And Dave is a Mormon—no offense, of course. I don't know. He is kind of gruff. Gruff?!? What am I saying?!! He's a barbarian in a letterman's jacket."

"Does Kat like Chris?" Jess said.

"You mean like him, or *like* him?" Tam said, jolted by Jess's question.

"Never mind."

"Oh, girl, don't you worry one bit about Kat. She's too much a Molly Mormon to get in your way. Besides, you got a year on her, and Kat will only marry an RM."

Jess wanted to ask what that meant, but Tam started sniggering about Dave again. Dave, Dave, Dave—he just *might* be a snazzy catch.

When they stopped in front of Jess's house, Tam asked her straight up. "You going to the meeting tonight?"

"What meeting?" Jess said, pushing a lock of hair over one ear.

Tam smiled and pointed a finger. "Don't *even* try playing dumb with me, sister. I know all your ins and outs. You haven't heard a word I said on the way home, 'cause you're thinking about Chris and this meeting tonight."

"Chris won't go," Jess said, "will he?"

"No way," said Tam. "I already talked to Dave, and Dave told me he'll beat the green-beans out Chris before letting him go to the Mormon Bashing tonight."

Jess looked at her house. She could see her father peeking out the window. "I'm surprised Dave won't be there."

"*He* just might be!" said Tam. "But if so, the cops will follow."

Shaking her head, Jess said, "That would only prove Professor Cooper's thesis about Mormons."

"Yeah, well, Dave is a sweetie, but he's not always been

the most exemplary member of the Church." She looked at the ceiling of her parent's car and sighed. "I think I could love him anyway."

Jess smirked and grinned and closed the car door. "Bye, hon."

"Bye, girl."

Then while deciding what to wear for the great Mormon Bashing, as Tam called it, Jess heard a car pull into her driveway and honk its horn.

Jess's father was taking a little after-dinner nap, or was at least pretending to. He was getting to be quite sneaky in his old age, so she second-guessed everything about him these days.

By the time Jess got to the door, Tam was back, her face white as a ghost. "We got to go, now! I drove by the church on Fig Street and it's already packing up."

"What do you mean *we* got to go now?" said Jess.

Tam stepped forward and grabbed her hand.

"I'm not dressed!" Jess looked down at her school outfit.

"Everyone's going to be there, Jess."

Jess pulled her to a stop. "You mean, Chris."

Tam yanked her forward again. "I mean *everyone*."

Chapter Twenty-Nine

Kat tried to stop them, but it didn't work so she came along for the ride, and to see what would happen.

Chris had never stepped into a non-LDS church before.

The building was old, its exterior made of dark wood that went up thirty feet to a pointed roof.

Inside the foyer, he saw bulletin boards announcing Bingo Night and this evening's appearance of Professor Diamond Cooper. In a photograph that had been glued a-tilt on a piece of blue poster board, Cooper smiled back, promising secrets with his eyes. The advertisement made him look like a lounge singer.

Beneath the bulletin boards, hundreds of fliers and little paper readers covered long tables with cartoon caricatures of Jesus and children.

Straight ahead, two large double doors stood open. Beyond them, Chris, Dave, and Kat saw a room packed with grumbling men and women in street clothes. It was standing room only, and Professor Cooper raised his voice to the stained glass windows more than once.

It was, "Mormon Scourge!" and "In *our* town!" and "Protect you from the Missionaries of a Religion of Sheep!"

"I've heard enough." Dave pushed past Chris.

"Wait." Chris caught him by the shoulder. "We have to do this right or we'll only make fools out of ourselves."

"This isn't going to work," said Kat, her voice trembling, her eyes wild with fear. "We've got to get *out* of here! Do you know what the bishop would say if he found out what you were doing?"

"Let's beat some heads," said Dave.

"No," Chris said. "We're supposed to be emissaries of peace."

"This is war, Chris and you know it!"

Chris hardened his eyes. "We go in calm. Or we don't go in at all."

"I told you not to come!" Dave said, fighting to keep his voice down to a whisper as he stabbed his finger into Chris's chest.

Kat pushed her face between theirs. "This isn't about you, Dave. And you don't have the weapons Chris has. *He's* an Elder."

That slapped Dave away. Almost nineteen years old, and already the idea of going on a mission had become a plague to him. And his sister loved to point out his every flaw.

Chris looked from Kat to Dave to the booming voice of Diamond Slick. "Let's go in."

* * *

As soon as they entered the room at the back of a long aisle leading right to the foot of the pulpit where the professor spoke, Cooper's face lit up with recognition.

He stopped speaking and grinned.

While Kat waited at the side of the entrance, Chris and Dave started slowly up the aisle.

"Well, well," said Cooper, his voice picking up a bit of a Southern twang. "Seems we have a couple of *Mormons* among us."

An old man to their right stood out of the congregation. He scowled in disdain at Chris and grabbed his wife to go.

Dave pointed one of his massive arms at the man and said, "Take a seat!"

The old man and woman sat in fear.

The mumbling of the crowd rumbled louder and two larger men stood, watched the biggest high school student carefully.

Dave squinted at them with angry eyes. "You came to hear about the *Mormon* Chris Noble, didn't you? The one Diamond Slick here wrote about in the paper?"

The two large men lifted their chins.

"Well here he is!"

Chris took another step forward, his eyes on the man behind the pulpit.

Can I do this? he thought. *Kat has NO IDEA how*

much I would like to leave. But right now … I need to stand for something bigger than myself. And I need to defend Jess, who got dragged into this.

"This is private property, young man," said Cooper with a grin. "We can have you arrested if you do not leave now. Or have you no respect for order in this great country?"

"Is that what you want?" said Chris. He turned to the congregation. "I suppose that would make a lot of you guys more comfortable, wouldn't it? It's much easier to talk behind someone's back than right in front of them. Talking in front of them … well, it makes gossip and hatred and fear feel a bit less *Christian*, doesn't it?"

"Last chance, Mr. Noble," said Cooper. "Go now, or we call the police."

More than a dozen cell phones appeared in upraised hands from the congregation to let the professor know they were ready to dial.

"Your remarks about me in the paper were not meant to draw me here?" said Chris taking another step closer to the pulpit. He stood halfway between Cooper and the exit now, and he stopped, turning a little to one side. "I think you *wanted* me to come, Professor Cooper. But if I was wrong, I'll be on my way. Let's go, Dave."

"No, no, son," said Cooper with a jovial laugh, a spider welcoming a fly to the web. He lifted a hand. "Come on in, *Chris Noble*. Actually, I *would* like to ask you a few questions."

The mumbling of the crowd turned to whispers so they could hear better. Still, it was difficult for them all to shut off their uncomfortable feelings. Chris wondered if some were not calling the cops anyway. Four or five couples sneaked out the far sides of the room, and Dave let them escape.

No matter how one looked at it, this wasn't going to be pretty, and everyone knew it.

The rest remained in their seats. *Why?* Chris wondered. *Curiosity? The ultimate in Real TV action? Blood? Or the humiliation of a future Mormon missionary?*

"Christopher Noble," said Professor Cooper with an air of grandeur. "Tell these good people the truth, if you can—"

Dave whispered into Chris's ear, "It's a court trial, not a church. Let's get this over with!"

Chris shushed him.

"—Are you in fact a member of the Church of Jesus Christ of Latter-day Saints?" said Cooper without weakening his ear-to-ear grin.

"You know I am," said Chris.

"And are you preparing for a mission?"

"Yes."

Cooper nodded. "Have you put in your papers?"

"I have."

"And when do you expect to hear back from Salt Lake City?"

Chris glanced around the crowd.

Why were they talking about this? He remembered suddenly a lesson from *The Book of Mormon*. When Zeezrom, a lawyer "expert in the devices of the devil", drilled Alma's missionary companion, Amulek, with questions before a population of good people, Zeezrom started out by speaking cordially and logically and getting him to answer questions with Yes, yes, yes. *It was the way of lawyers,* Chris's seminary teacher had said.

Now that Chris was on the receiving end of the same tactic, he wasn't so sure of himself anymore. Would Cooper steer Chris into a corner if possible? If so, *then* would appear the sticks sharpened at both ends for piercing.

"When did I get my call?"

"His *call*," said Professor Cooper to the congregation so that they heard it. "You already got it *in the mail*, Chris?"

"On Saturday," said Chris.

Cooper nodded. "And where does it say you're going?"

"Northern Japan."

"Exotic! And did someone receive a *revelation* to send you to Japan?"

Chris swallowed. "Yes." It was the truth. Not only did he believe it, he trusted in it, because when it came to foreign languages, he could hardly pass a class. Since graduating from high school less than a year ago, he had already forgotten just about everything he'd learned in two years of Spanish—except *Me llamo Juan.*

"Do you have experience in Japanese?" said Cooper.

"No."

"But it will help you get the girls later, won't it?"

Blinking, Chris wasn't sure he had heard correctly. It wasn't one of the questions he had anticipated in this line of thought. "I'm sorry?"

"The girls, Christopher." Cooper grinned again. "We all know how much you like girls. Everyone in this room saw your picture in the paper!"

"That was—"

"Tell us, Mr. Noble," Cooper said, "isn't it true that Mormon girls after high school are partial to RMs?" He leaned on the pulpit as if sharing a secret with the crowd. "For the rest of us, that's a Mormon code for 'Returned Missionary.'"

Chris didn't say anything. When Korihor argued with Alma in *The Book of Mormon*, he actually sounded like the underdog, a simple sincere guy who was trying to teach the truth to the people while Alma smashed him with words. While answering all of Alma's questions, he came off honest and straight forward, and repeated over and over his one devastating question, which seemed to prove his point: If Alma could not show him a sign, then God must not exist.

But Alma had been the smart one by turning things around. He put the burden of proof onto Korihor's shoulders: *What evidence have YOU that there is no God?*

Korihor could never answer.

Here in the Church of the 1st Resurrection, Chris still didn't know what to say. Should he just interrupt Professor Cooper? If he did, wouldn't the people just throw him out?

Dave was right. He shouldn't have come. By standing here, he represented not only the youth of the Church of Jesus Christ of Latter-day Saints, but everyone who believed in the Restoration and *The Book of Mormon*.

He wasn't ready for this.

"Come on, Chris," said Cooper after a stretch of silence. "Don't all the Mormon girls hanker after RM boys?"

"Generally," said Chris.

"And isn't *that* why you are going on your mission?" Cooper's voice snapped loud and quick. "Tell us the truth!"

"No!" Chris answered fast, the din of mumbling and whispering around him increasing.

"You're not going on your mission to become some prize for a good Mormon girl?" said Cooper.

"Of course not," said Chris. He was going into the field to serve the Lord.

Cooper leaned close to the microphone and spoke in a soft voice. "But didn't you just agree that that's what the *good* LDS girls want?"

Did I? Chris thought. Everything was getting a little too confusing for him. He didn't know where this was leading. It went too fast, and he could sense the canyon floor rising up to meet him in the face.

Squinting, Cooper said, "You don't *care* about the good Mormon girls, do you Chris. You're already making out with a Catholic woman before your long journey. Isn't lasciviousness a sin in your religion?"

"Jess has nothing to do with this," said Chris.

From behind, Dave grabbed his arm.

The crowd mentioned things like, "Our daughters" and "Sleeping around" and "Not so righteous, is he!"

"You can't even *marry* a girl who isn't a Mormon," said Cooper. "Isn't that true?"

"Not in the Temple, no," Chris said, forced to raise his voice over the roll of verbal thunder all around him.

"So you're only *using* that young lady in the picture like a filthy man uses a prostitute," said Cooper.

"No!" said Chris, though no one was listening to him now.

"And how, pray tell, do *you* think that young Catholic woman would feel if she knew that your flings with her are but a moment? That you intended to leave her from the start? You *knew* you would not marry her? That she is *only a tall drink of water before you head off across a two-year desert of celibacy?*"

"It's not like that!" Chris yelled over the other voices.

Cooper raised his hands, and like Moses, stilled the waters. The room went quiet. He hung on tight to the pulpit and leaned forward. "Well, Christopher Noble … why don't we ask *her*."

Chris's eyes blew wide.

Behind him, Dave said, "Ah, shoot."

Diamond Cooper turned his wide grin to the left side of the congregation. "*Jessica Singer!* Won't you please stand up?"

As nervous as a small animal surrounded by wolves, Jess rose out of the crowd.

Chapter Thirty

Jess and Tam had arrived in time for the beginning of Professor Cooper's anti-Mormon preaching. The local pastor had introduced him, and at first there had only been a lot of talk of love and peace and harmony. The change to the fire-and-brimstone burning Mormons had been so subtle, she almost hadn't noticed it.

To remain inconspicuous until they found the others, Jess had moved them through the crowd to the side of the chapel where a number of others stood. She thought Diamond Cooper, who sat on the stand, had seen her, but she wasn't sure, and she didn't know if he would recognize her face in the hundreds of others thronging the room.

A nice man with a full red beard had seen them standing as the introductions were given. He'd offered them the chair on which he sat as well as the one he'd saved beside it. They waved him away as politely as possible. When he stood and slid out of the row, for them, smiling all the while, Jess realized that if she and Tam didn't take the seats, someone else would.

Besides, they hadn't spotted Chris and the others yet.

Maybe they were hiding. Maybe they hadn't arrived yet.

When Chris entered, Tam almost jumped out of her chair. Jess had held her down. None of the others knew she was there, let alone Chris, and she didn't want to mess him up. It was no secret that he was a mouse walking into a den of serpents.

As Cooper fired his questions and steered Chris into a trap, Jess had to almost sit on Tam to keep her in her chair. She covered Tam's mouth and knew she wouldn't be able to hold her for long.

But when Cooper swung his eyes down her row and locked them right onto Jess's face, Tam froze.

Jess stood, thinking about what he and Chris had said.

Cooper had basically called her a harlot in front of all these people. Or rather, he'd said that Chris was using her for a bit of fun and pleasure before he dropped her cold and went to Japan.

In her heart, she knew that wasn't true.

In her mind, she couldn't argue at all.

"Welcome, Jessica, to the Church of the 1st Resurrection. I realize you're a Catholic and therefore not accustomed to our ways—I can respect that," said Cooper, offering his long grin. "I am sure you had no idea how a young Mormon fellow might *use* a pretty girl like you."

Chris took a step closer to the pulpit. "You leave her alone."

Raising his eyebrows at Chris and the congregation, Professor Cooper said, "Why don't we just let Jessica speak for herself, shall we?" He pursed his lips. "Or are you afraid of what she might say?"

A stir of whispers started again, but this time half the eyes clung to Jess.

She slid out of the row to the wall. "I didn't come here to listen to you, Professor Cooper."

"No?" he said. She could see on his playful face that he didn't really care why she had come at all. *He* was the one using her in his anti-Mormon campaign.

"I came to hear what Chris had to say."

He nodded. "That's fair! Isn't it, good people of Harmon, California? And why shouldn't Jessica *hear* what Chris has to say. There have been lies enough. He has touched her, used her, and intends to abuse her by sucking her dry of kisses and then leaving for a foreign land … so that he can *marry a Mormon* girl when he gets back!"

"You *wanted* me here," said Chris to the man behind the pulpit. "Was it only to spread lies and exaggerations?"

"Absolutely not," said Cooper. "I stand before these good people to teach them the truth about the Mormon character."

"What do you really know about Mormons?" Chris said.

Cooper ignored the question. "Isn't it true, Mr. Noble, that as a young man preparing for a mission, you are supposed to be leading an exemplary life? Isn't that what a missionary is supposed to be? A representative of a higher power? Do you *stand* for anything? Or are all these platitudes nothing more than pretty words passed from Mormon to Mormon for their neighbors to hear, so that one day they too might follow like dumb sheep?"

Jess watched Chris think for a while.

Everyone waited for his answers.

Chris's eyes darted toward Jess, but wouldn't lock onto her. "In this case," he said at last, "I would prefer to follow the example of the Shepherd."

"Oh really?" said Cooper.

"Yeah," said Chris. "I believe the Bible to be the word of God—"

"As far as it is translated *correctly*," Cooper added, clarifying for the masses that Mormons might pick and choose which parts they want to believe and discard.

"In the New Testament," Chris said, "a bunch of guys tried to trap Jesus with words. So I'm saying what he said: I'll answer your questions, Cooper, if you will first answer one of mine."

All heads turned from Chris Noble to Diamond Cooper.

Cooper's eyes jerked left and right over the congregation. Grabbing hold of Chris again, he tossed up a hand and said, "Well go ahead then! Ask your question."

Chris started walking forward again. "Is it all right … for a man professing the word of God—you in this case—to break the law?" From his jacket, he pulled a manila envelope out of his jacket.

Necks stretched to see better.

Chairs creaked as people shifted in their seats.

Jess lifted herself on her toes.

Cooper cocked his head to one side. "What are you talking about?"

Having arrived at the foot of the pulpit, Chris reached into the folder, but left his hand there as he turned to face the congregation without a microphone.

The room went silent.

"Good people. You have all learned the great Mormon secret," said Chris. He smiled a little and raised his eyebrows. "We are human. Just like you." He looked at those who had been lucky enough to get a seat in the wooden pews that made up the front fifteen rows of the chapel. "We need a Savior, even Jesus Christ, just like you."

"No one came to hear *you* preach, boy!" said Cooper.

Jess filled her lungs with air and let it out with a high-pitched wail of words. "Why don't you let him speak! Or are *you* afraid, *Mr.* Cooper?"

Chris met her eyes.

Go on! she said with a nod.

"If you hate us," said Chris, "because we try to practice high standards, some of which—like not smoking or drinking, and spreading the word of the Lord like Paul and Peter and John the beloved—you yourselves have had thoughts about practicing ... if you hate members of the Church of Jesus Christ of Latter-day Saints, then you pose one question: Who is the God of Hate?"

The god of what? Jess said in her mind.

"Who wants contention spread among the children of men?" Chris said.

Chris waited for people to answer. No one was looking at Jess anymore. They all squirmed or held their breath silent, uncomfortable, and a few gazed at the man behind the pulpit to bail them out.

"As for you, Mr. Cooper," said Chris. From the manila folder, he withdrew a small stack of papers stapled together on one side. "Jess's father asked me to deliver this to you in person."

Whose father? Jess thought.

Jess's father, Chris had said.

"It's a lawsuit," said Chris after placing the papers into Diamond Cooper's hands. Chris shrugged. "Libel, slander, and defamation of character, that sort of thing. You ought to have a lawyer read it, to inform you of your rights before trial."

Cooper's face turned white as he examined the documents. He drew his mouth into a tiny O shape, and from his eyes, Jess could tell he was completely lost.

As Chris started back toward Dave and the exit, Cooper's voice flared again. "Jess's *father* did you say?"

Chris turned and gave a nod. "He's a lawyer."

"And you're *using* him too?" said Cooper. "That's two Catholics for the price of one. You Mormons really know how to do your math."

My father?!? thought Jess. *And CHRIS?*

Chris was no longer swayed. He stood tall and heroic against Cooper's gaze of confusion and panting anger. "Mr. Singer might not approve of my relationship with Jess. But he likes it less when grownups use young people in illegal ways to further their personal agendas."

Scrunching the summons and complaint into a crinkling rod of paper, Cooper waved it in the air. "This isn't slander, boy!"

Chris shook his head. "You can explain that to the judge. Mr. Singer's handling my complaint from now on. I won't be around to hear your whining anymore. Let's get out of here, Dave."

Before he made it to the door, Chris turned to see Tam clamoring over the innocents who had come to listen. "Out of my way!"

But his eyes sought out Jess, and she hadn't moved.
Why?
He loves me, she thought.
And he is using me.
"Jess?" he called.

Hundreds of eyes turned to look at her.

"Well, Jessica?" said Cooper with the last bit of cool he could pull together. "You've heard the truth? Is it time to go all mushy? Are you going to put your brain aside and charge after him so he can feast on your face until he's ready to abandon you? You *know* what I say is true!"

"That's it," said Dave. He charged the pulpit.

Before he got four steps, Chris had him by both shoulders. "We've done our part," he said.

Dave didn't take his hard eyes off of Diamond Slick. "I haven't done mine."

"But if you did," Jess could barely hear Chris say, "you'd be just like him."

With fists tight against his sides, Dave stared Cooper down for a few seconds more, then left the building.

Tam caught up with Kat in the doorway to the chapel.

Chris looked at Jess one more time. With a soft voice, he said, "Let's go."

"Yes," said Cooper. "Go be his harlot."

She looked at him.

"Don't stare at me. Go!" He leaned hard against the pulpit. "If that's all you're good for, then what does it matter?" After righting himself and sighing at the microphone without taking his eyes off of her, he said, "I guess you'll have to decide right here and now just what sort of person you really are, Jessica Singer."

Everyone was watching her.

Chris had lifted a hand over half of the congregation, reaching for her, motioning with his fingers for her to come with him.

"I—" She couldn't speak.

Since Thursday night—not even a full week!—it had all been such whirlwind.

Would she end up in the paper tomorrow?

Was that the click of a camera somewhere in the congregation, trapping her thin form against a chapel wall for all to squint over and comment about later?

Those questions didn't matter.

She had decisions to make.

Only one, really.

So what did she need to know?

Do I love him?

Yes.

Does Chris really love me at all?

I—

Would he have put me through all this, if he really cared?

He tried not to. He didn't think anything would happen. He spent years looking away. He couldn't help himself ... because he does *love me.*

But he's leaving.

Yes.

So he's using you.

No.

Then ... what IS he doing?

Chris is ... he is ... doing the same thing I've been doing.

And what's that?

Hoping.

She licked her lips. Her voice came out scratchy, but loud enough for everyone to hear. And as she spoke, she kept her eyes on Chris. Because no one else really mattered.

"I love him. I'm not going to let him out of my sight until the day he leaves for Japan. And when he goes," she said, lifting her chin, her voice wavering, "I'm going to wait for him."

Cooper's voice was equally soft, and even sounded sincere, though she didn't turn to look at him. "You're going to wait. Even though he will only marry a Mormon? Does that mean you intend to become one?"

She shut her mouth. "That's for me to decide. I have a little less than four weeks with you," she said to Chris. "I'm not going to waste a day."

Chapter Thirty-One

"This is for you," Chris said. He opened her hand, placed a small pink box with a bow on her palm, and then closed her fingers over the gift.

Jess smiled. They had spent every day together until this moment, and they had been the most wonderful days of her life.

"What is it?" she said.

Standing close enough to kiss her again, he shrugged one shoulder and said, "A little something for you to hang onto while I'm away."

"Oh, this is so beautiful!" said Tam, weeping through her shining smile.

"Yeah," Dave told her. "But do you have to stare? Come on." He took her arm and guided her to the other side of the chapel.

"So what did you think of your first Sacrament Meeting?" said Kat.

Chris ignored her, and Jess was thankful his eyes didn't leave hers.

It wasn't like Jess was counting the hours that remained

before Chris's departure.

"I wouldn't have missed your farewell talk for the world," Jess said to Chris. "It really moved me."

Truth was, in her mind, if Chris was so devoted to serving the Lord, she knew he would be an equally loyal and dedicated husband.

Not that she was thinking marriage.

Not that she *wasn't*. After all, what girl *didn't* think of her boyfriend standing some day beside her in a tux … or whatever they wore in the Temple.

These were all questions she would deal with at a later time.

It was like Chris had said in his talk: *We just have to have faith. Faith is believing, even when a lack of evidence makes what you want to believe in seem impossible.*

Chris shot Kat a gentle glance.

"Okay," said Kat with a jovial voice, getting the message. She curtsied in her pretty dress and disappeared back into the chapel.

"Are you going to open it?" said Chris.

He would report at the MTC, which Jess learned stood for Missionary Training Center, on Wednesday at noon.

They still had a couple days left before, as he explained, he would be ordained a missionary and be unable to see her romantically.

But he would write. He'd promised that. He said missionaries *live* for letters from home.

"You don't want me to wait until—"

"Open it now," he said.

She grinned again and pulled off the white bow. After removing the small box top, she handed it to him and parted the tissue paper.

Inside the clouds of white, she saw a short cylinder made of silver. At the top, a key ring had been attached. Along the side of the metal, she saw the words, HOLD TO THE ROD.

She withdrew the object. Without trying to open it, she said, "How do you get the oil out."

He chuckled. "You mean like this vial?" From his pocket, Chris drew out his own keys and held them up. There, on a silver cylinder that was far thicker, she saw where the top of the container connected the rest to his key ring. "Only Elders have these."

"But ... Dave—"

"Dave won't become an Elder until he turns nineteen next month." He felt the letters etched into the rod. "I love you, Jess. This is to help you remember ... to choose the right, no matter what the future holds."

I hope it holds you, she thought.

His eyes seemed to say, *I hope it does too.*

"I'll remember," Jess said. "I'll remember forever."

He swallowed, shutting his eyes and opening them again. "Jess ... I ... I can't ask you to wait for me."

"No. You can't," she said. "But you can always hope."

Chris grinned.

Jess rose up on her toes, and kissed him.

JAMES STEIMLE is the ultimate hopeless romantic. To charm the girl of his dreams into marrying him, he wrote and produced a leather-bound fantasy novel, pulling out all the stops—a love letter tour de force.

James Steimle is an award-winning writer of stories that have been printed, reprinted, anthologizes, received additional honorable mentions in additional anthologies, and appeared in magazines across the United States, Canada, and Europe.

He is the eclectic author of *The Kukulkan Manuscript* (intellectual thriller), *The Room That Wasn't There* (historical ghost story), *The Ghost People* (anthropological adventure), *Interference* (science fiction), as well as his Halloween bestseller for children, *The Autumn Land*.

Readers are encouraged to visit and send James e-mail at his website, www.steimle.us.

www.ingramcontent.com/pod-product-compliance
Lightning Source LLC
Chambersburg PA
CBHW071127170626
46809CB00002B/528